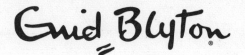

House at the Corner

AWARD PUBLICATIONS LIMITED

For further information on Enid Blyton please visit *www.blyton.com*

ISBN 978-1-84135-647-1

Illustrated by Eric Rowe
Cover illustration by Leo Hartas

Illustrations © Award Publications Limited

First published 1947 by Lutterworth Press
First published by Award Publications Limited 1999
This edition first published 2010

Published by Award Publications Limited,
The Old Riding School, The Welbeck Estate,
Worksop, Nottinghamshire, S80 3LR

12 2

Printed in Germany

Contents

1

Aunt Grace comes to Stay

Old Aunt Grace was going to stay with her relations, the Farrells. She sat in the train, surrounded by her belongings.

Every now and again she counted them over. 'My big brown bag. My little blue one. Sukie. My umbrella and sunshade. My electric kettle. My mackintosh. My odds and ends. Yes, they're all there.'

The odds and ends were tied together with string. They were the things that Aunt Grace had decided to take with her at the last minute, after her bags were packed and locked – a packet of sunflower seeds for Sukie, her parrot, a magazine and a book, a tin of toffees and a packet of sandwiches, and a few fading flowers from her garden.

'Yes, they're all there,' said the old lady and closed her sharp eyes, trying to sleep. But she couldn't sleep. She thought of the Farrells one by one – John Farrell the father, Lucy the mother, and all the five children.

And if that stuck-up Pam tries any of her high-and-mighty ways on me this time, she'll be sorry, thought the old lady, grimly. And as for that boy, Tony, what he wants is a good spanking – always did. Lizzie's the only one worth anything in that family. The twins are always too busy with this and that to know properly.

She thought of all the five children. She was a sharp-eyed, sharp-witted old lady who didn't at all mind saying what she thought. She went from one to the other of her relations, staying a month here and a week there, giving everyone what she called 'a piece of her mind' if she thought they needed it. But she could be kind too, and though many of them feared her, some of her relations loved her and knew there was a great deal more to her than her sharp eyes and tongue.

Let me see now, she thought, as she sat with her eyes half-closed, it's nearly a year since I saw the Farrell children. They will have grown! My, Pam must be almost ready to leave school. Time she came home and helped her mother a bit, I think. Doesn't even know how to make a bed properly!

She gave a little snort, remembering how untidy Pamela was, and how she forgot things, and how she never could sew on a button that came off. Aunt Grace was as neat as a new pin, and even now could embroider beautifully without her glasses.

'Ah,' she said, sitting up, 'there's the house now, on the corner there. I always like that first glimpse of it.'

The train always passed by the Farrells' house, half a mile before it reached the station. Aunt Grace looked at it and her eyes softened. She loved 'House at the Corner', as it was called. She had spent a great deal of her own childhood there. There it stood, on a corner, facing the hills, an old rambling house, big and lovely, moss growing here and there on its old red tiles. Round it spread a garden as rambling as the house itself, full of flowers.

'It's a lovely house,' said old Aunt Grace, 'and a lovely garden. I'm glad to be going to stay there again. Maybe I'm not very welcome – too sharp-tongued, and I know Lucy doesn't like Sukie the parrot – but they can put up with me for a little while!'

The train ran into the station. Aunt Grace began to gather up her things. She leaned out of the window and called the porter to take the parrot's big cage. Sukie, who was always too frightened to utter even the smallest squawk when on a train, came to life and scratched her poll.

'Porter!' she said, in a voice so like Aunt Grace's that the old porter jumped. 'Hey, porter!'

Aunt Grace climbed out of the carriage and looked to see who had come to meet her. How nice if the whole family had come! That would be a welcome indeed.

At first it looked as if not one of the Farrell family was there to greet her. The old lady frowned. Then she caught sight of a girl of about sixteen coming towards her, a plain, rather gawky girl, with glasses on her nose and wire round her front teeth to keep them straight.

'Lizzie!' said Aunt Grace. 'How you've grown! My, I'd hardly have known you!'

Lizzie smiled and showed the wire round her teeth. She had nice teeth but they stuck too far forward and the dentist was trying to put them right for her, but how Lizzie hated that wire round them! She hated wearing glasses too, but since she had had measles her eyes had been weak, and she had to wear the glasses.

'Where are the others?' said Aunt Grace, collecting the odds and ends. 'Too busy to bother about their old aunt, I suppose?'

This was exactly right, but Lizzie couldn't say so, of course. Nobody had wanted to come and meet Aunt Grace.

'Old bore!' Pam had said. 'Always descending on people that don't want her. I'm not going to meet her!'

Tony had simply disappeared. He knew so

well how to do that when he didn't want to do anything.

The twins had argued so heatedly about going to the station to meet Aunt Grace that their mother had given in and said they needn't go. So there was only Lizzie left, and, as usual, she was the one to do something that nobody else would do. So there she was at the station, smiling her shy smile and helping her great-aunt with her luggage.

Lizzie had a taxi outside and they got into it, Sukie looking disgusted at the idea of another trip on wheels. She hunched herself up and shut her eyes.

'Sukie will be glad to be home,' said Aunt Grace. 'She hates journeys. So do I.'

'You make so many journeys, don't you, Aunt Grace?' said Lizzie. 'Always going here and there. If you hate them so much, why don't you get a little cottage of your own and settle there with Sukie? Then you wouldn't always have to be packing and unpacking, and travelling in trains and taxis!'

Aunt Grace looked at Lizzie sharply, wondering if the girl was hinting that a cottage home would prevent Aunt Grace from imposing herself so much on her relations. But she saw that Lizzie was not thinking that at all. The girl's warm brown eyes were candid and kind, not sly or mischievous as Pam and Tony's so often were.

'Well,' said Aunt Grace, with a funny little sigh, 'I'm afraid of living alone, with my thoughts and memories, Lizzie. I've made a lot of mistakes in my life and I remember them when I'm alone. I'm a lonely old woman and I want life and friends around me – yes, even if people don't want me, I still want to be with them!'

Lizzie didn't know what to say. She had never thought of Aunt Grace feeling lonely. Her great-aunt was so talkative, so fond of arranging other people's lives for them, so full of this, that and the other – how could she ever feel lonely? She looked in surprise at the old lady. Aunt Grace patted her hand.

'You're a nice child,' she said, unexpectedly. 'Not enough go in you, that's your trouble. Do everybody else's dirty work. Don't think enough of yourself!'

'Well – Pam's the pretty one, and the clever one,' said Lizzie, loyally. 'I'll never be pretty and I'm not very clever, I'm afraid. And I'm scared of people, and of trying anything new! I wish I could be like Pam.'

'Now don't you wish that!' began Aunt Grace, and then stopped. It wouldn't do to tell Lizzie what she thought of vain, conceited, clever Pam, with her hard little mouth and sarcastic tongue. No, it wouldn't do.

'Here we are,' said Lizzie as the taxi stopped, and she opened the door. The taxi-driver got down and began to pull out the luggage. Lizzie's mother came running down to the gate.

'Aunt Grace! Welcome to House at the Corner!' she said. 'Come along in. Greta will bring in your things with Lizzie.'

Greta, the housekeeper, came out, beaming. She was an Austrian, kind, generous and hot-tempered. Tomorrow she would be fuming and raging because of something Aunt Grace had said – but at this minute she was full of warm welcome, very pleasant to see.

'It is vairy nice to see you again, Madame,' she said, smiling all over her jolly, plump face. 'I help Miss Lizzie wiz your zings.'

'Thank you, Greta,' said Aunt Grace, and went indoors with her niece. Lizzie and Greta struggled in with the bags, and then went out again to fetch Sukie the parrot in her big cage.

'Zis parrot I do not like,' said Greta in a loud whisper to Lizzie. 'She has an ugly voice, she go sqwook, sqwook all the time. Why does not your aunt have a nice fat little cat or a good, good dog?'

Lizzie laughed. 'Oh, I think a parrot is good fun,' she said. 'Won't the twins be pleased to see Sukie again? They love her! They taught her to say all kinds of things last time.'

'Polly put the kattle on,' said Sukie, at once.

'Kettle, not kattle,' said Lizzie. 'Yes, the twins taught you to say that, didn't they, Sukie? Good Polly!'

'Poor poor Polly,' said Sukie, cheerfully, very glad to think that she would at last be able to stand on a firm floor again, instead of on things on wheels that jolted and jerked all the time.

Aunt Grace had been taken up to her room by Mrs Farrell. Lizzie had put vases of fresh flowers there, and the sun came in at the open windows. Aunt Grace sat down on the bed.

'This was always my room when I was a child,' she said, as she had said so many times before. 'It's nice of you to remember that, Lucy. There's a new wallpaper, of course, and a new carpet, but the view is just the same, and the apple tree outside the window is the very same one!'

Mrs Farrell had heard this so many times that she hardly needed to listen. She smiled at the tired old lady. 'Yes, I knew you'd like Lizzie's room,' she said. 'Lizzie turned out for you, and went into the spare room.'

'Nice child,' said Aunt Grace, shaking some lavender water on to her handkerchief and mopping her forehead with it. 'Nice child – but very plain, Lucy. Must she wear those glasses still, and that wire round her teeth?'

'Just a little while longer,' said Mrs Farrell.

'Yes, poor Lizzie – she doesn't shine beside Pam, I'm afraid. Pam's so very pretty and so smart too.'

'Handsome is as handsome does!' said Aunt Grace. 'Well, I'll have a little rest before lunch, my dear, if you don't mind. I'll see the rest of the children then, if they're in. Or maybe they're keeping out of my way?'

This was the kind of sly thing that Aunt Grace so often said, and that was very near the truth. Mrs Farrell laughed a little and reddened.

'You'll see them all at lunch-time,' she said. 'You won't know the twins! They've grown so. They're wrapped up in one another, of course, just as they always were – have the same likes and dislikes, and go their own way. I don't really feel that I know very much about them!'

She went out of the room and shut the door quietly. Aunt Grace took off her shoes and dress, drew back the bedspread and lay down, sniffing at her lavender-scented handkerchief.

'I expect Lizzie grumbled at having to turn out of her room,' she said to herself. 'But it's nice to be back again in the place I know. Yes, it's nice to be back.'

2

The Five Farrell Children

It was the Easter holidays. They were almost over, and soon all the five Farrell children would go back to school. The twins hated that because it meant that they were parted all day. David went to the big grammar school for boys, and Delia, his twin, went to the same big girls' school as her elder sisters, Lizzie and Pam. Tony, her elder brother, went to the grammar school with David.

Now all five children were in their big play-room downstairs, waiting for Greta to bang the gong for lunch.

'Is she here?' asked Tony, coming in last.

'Who? Aunt Grace?' asked Pam. 'Yes, she's here all right, worse luck. Going to put everyone in their places as usual, I suppose. Well, she won't put me! I'm seventeen and a half, almost grown up, going to college in September – she can't order me about any longer.'

'She jolly well won't order me about, either,' said Tony.

'She will. You're only fourteen,' said Pam.

'I may be only fourteen, but I'm as tall as

17

you,' said Tony. He was. He looked about seventeen, with his fine tall body and big shoulders. He was a handsome, well-built boy and Mrs Farrell was very proud of him. He was as clever as Pam, and had just as good a memory and could as easily be top of his form as Pam was of hers, but he preferred to play the fool and make the others laugh. 'Plenty of time to work hard when I want a scholarship,' he said when his father wanted to know why he was so low in form. 'I could lick all the others easily if I wanted to. I'll work hard as soon as I get into old Snorty's form, Dad. I'll have to.'

He *would* have to. The master there was what the boys called a snorter, a hard-driving, determined man, anxious to make the very best of his boys' brains. But the master of the form below him was Blinky, or Mr Holmes, a short-sighted, mild-tempered master on whom the boys played endless tricks. Tony had great fun in Blinky's class, lazed his time away, played jokes and tricks, and altogether enjoyed himself.

'Still,' said Mrs Farrell, who was far too proud of her tall son, 'he's only fourteen. He's got good brains. He'll work hard as soon as he has to. It's his master's fault for being so easy-going.'

She spoilt both Tony and Pam. Pam had always been so pretty and so clever. She had really never needed to work hard for anything, for her good brains put her at the top of her form and kept her there without much effort. Pam was proud of her looks and her brains. She meant to do well in the world!

I shall win my scholarship, go to college and do brilliantly there! she thought as she looked at herself in her mirror, seeing the deep blue eyes, the wavy golden hair and the long, curly eyelashes. She didn't see the hard little mouth that spoilt her pretty face, nor the little frown lines that told of bad temper. She only saw a very pretty face, clever and attractive. I shall do very well at college and then I shall take a fine job somewhere, and make a lot of money, and then I shall marry a very rich man, and have poor old Lizzie to stay with me, she thought.

Nobody thought much of Lizzie. It was partly her own fault because she would hide herself away so much. She was shy of visitors, shy at parties, shy of going out anywhere. She thought herself so plain and stupid – why should anyone want to talk to her or make friends with her?

She had never been brilliant at school, except in her literature class. There she always had good marks – but what was the good of being first in only one subject if you were never above the middle in all the others? It only made people say that you gave too much time to literature and not enough to things like arithmetic or geography.

But Lizzie was kind and patient with others in a way that Pam and Tony would never try to be. She did not talk very much herself, but other people liked to talk to her. They told her all about themselves.

Old Mrs Twitchen down the lane told her about the children she had had and what had happened to them all. It was like a story to Lizzie. The woman in the sweetshop told her about the cats she had had – every one of the thirteen she had kept during her long life – and they came alive for Lizzie, and she listened so patiently that Miss Cullen loved her and had always given her more sweets for her money than any of the other children. Even now Lizzie slipped into the little shop to see Miss Cullen's latest cat. He was a Manx and had no tail, and

the tale of his misdeeds would have filled a book.

The twins, David and Delia, were always wrapped up in their own affairs. They were ten years old and seemed real babies to the others. Pam had no time for them at all.

'Always bringing in half-dead birds and keeping smelly caterpillars and horrible mice!' she would say.

'Well, didn't you, when you were our age?' demanded David. 'Have you forgotten?'

'Don't be cheeky, now,' said Pam. 'No, of course I didn't do the awful things you do. Catch me keeping mice!'

'You're silly, you're afraid of mice,' said Delia. 'You think you're wonderful, Pam, but you don't even know the names of the commonest wild flowers or birds, and you don't know the difference between a swede and a turnip!'

'Well, who wants to?' said Pam, annoyed. 'You and your nature lore and your gardening! You make me tired. Why don't you play proper games like *we* used to. You've always got your heads in bird books, or are collecting weeds or hobnobbing with old Frost the gardener, pretending to help him!'

'We don't pretend. We do help him,' said David. 'You ought to see how our lettuces are coming on, under the cloches! You'll be having early salad soon, and when you do, you jolly well think of all the hard work Delia and I have done in the garden. You never do a thing. You don't even make your own bed.'

'Shut up,' said Pam, angrily. 'I won't have you talking to me like that. I'll smack you both!'

The twins spoke the truth when they said that they really did help Frost and didn't just pretend. They both had a real passion for out-of-doors, for flowers and birds and animals, and for gardening. Frost was getting old and he needed help in the big garden. So the twins had come to his aid, and worked as hard as any gardener in the holidays and whenever they could spare the time during term.

'It amuses them!' said Mrs Farrell, who could not seem to think of the twins as anything but children just out of infant school. 'I hope they won't get in Frost's way, that's all!'

She didn't know all they did out there in the garden. She hadn't seen David using Frost's heavy spade valiantly for an hour at a time. She didn't know how Delia spent a whole evening reading all Frost's old flower catalogues. She hadn't heard the questions the twins asked the gardener, or seen the delight in the old fellow's eyes as he patiently explained this and that to the solemn pair before him.

'They're the only ones that take any interest!' he told his wife. 'Pam never even sees me or the garden. Tony, he only thinks I'm somebody to play his silly jokes on. Tied a bit of string to a paintpot, he did, the other day, and when I opened the shed door, the string pulled the paint all over my feet. Ho, he thought that was a fine joke, he did – wasting his father's paint and spoiling my boots!'

'He's a bad boy,' said Mrs Frost. 'Spoilt too. Lizzie's the one for me. She listens to my old tales as patient as you please. I've told her all the old tales my granny told me, and old they must be for my gran got them from her gran. Ah, my gran was a fine storyteller, she was!'

'Oh, Lizzie's all right,' said old Frost. 'Got a lot more in her than folks think. But she's so shy . . . like . . . like a little bird that flies off as soon as you look at it. And the others just make her do what they want her to do. She's too weak with them, she is. Why, she'll soon have those twins ordering her about! You should have seen them today, cleaning out the greenhouse with me. Good as any gardeners, they was!'

'You're real set on those twins, aren't you?' said old Mrs Frost. 'And I'm real set on Lizzie. But I've no time for the other two. And what's more I know someone else who's got no time for them, either. And that's their great-aunt, that's just come to stay! Ha, she'll put them in their place all right!'

But it was growing difficult to put either Pam or Tony 'in their place' now. Even Aunt Grace would find that out. Pam felt herself to be almost grown up, and Tony could not check his cheeky tongue. Only with his father was he really polite now. Always teasing, always laughing, always up to some joke or other, Tony, in his own words 'had a good time' from morning to night, looked up to by the other boys of his class, feared by Blinky, the master of his form, and admired by all the smaller boys – except David, his small brother, three forms below him.

David had no time for Tony. Solemn, serious David thought scornfully of him. Tony teased David and Delia unmercifully, labelled them babies, set their pet mice free and threatened to

give their silkworms to Sukie the parrot. The twins retired into themselves and seemed to cut themselves completely off from their family, living in a little world of their own.

This was the family that Aunt Grace had come to visit. She had loved them all when they were little. Now they were growing up. Her fingers itched to meddle with them and set them right. She knew she shouldn't interfere. She had made up her mind not to, whatever happened. But she wasn't at all sure she would be able to keep her word!

The lunch gong sounded, banged vigorously by Greta. The children trooped out of the playroom into the dining-room. Mrs Farrell was there and she beamed at them.

'Have you w—' she began, but Tony interrupted her.

'Mother, have you washed your hands and done your hair?' he said, cheekily. 'Did you wipe your shoes when you came in?'

The others laughed. Tony was cheeky, but it did sound so funny.

'Here's Aunt Grace,' said his mother as the old lady came hurrying into the room, her grey, wavy hair neatly brushed.

'Well, my dears,' she said, 'here's your tiresome old great-aunt back again. Pam, child, you look quite grown up! And bless us all, is this

Tony? Why, Tony, you're a head above me! And I remember you a squalling baby in your pram! I've seen you, Lizzie dear – and here are the twins! It's a good thing you're boy and girl, or I should never be able to tell you apart!'

The greetings over, the family sat down to their meal. Lizzie helped her mother with the serving. It was on the tip of Aunt Grace's tongue to ask why Pam didn't help too, but she stopped herself in time.

'What delicious greens,' she said as Lizzie took off the lid of one of the vegetable dishes.

'*We* helped to grow them!' said David proudly.

'You must show me round the garden, David,' said Aunt Grace, remembering how interested the twins were in gardening. 'Oh, it's good to be back with you all. We're going to have a good time together, aren't we?'

'Yes, Aunt Grace,' said Lizzie. But she was the only one who answered!

3

Lizzie – and Elizabeth

The household soon settled down to having Aunt Grace in its midst. For the first day or two the children were more or less on their best behaviour. Pam did not give herself quite so many airs and graces. Tony was a little more polite than usual. Lizzie ran round Aunt Grace and waited on her as much as she could. The twins included her in their conversation, and even took her round the garden, being pleasantly surprised at all the things she knew about it.

'You forget I was a child here too, like you,' said the old lady. 'Why, I remember the time before that railway bridge was over there – and do you see that hill? In my day it was covered with trees. But they've been cut down now.'

The twins listened politely. They had heard all this before. Aunt Grace saw their faces and stopped.

'I've told you all that before, haven't I?' she said. 'Well, well - you're at least polite enough to listen, which is more than I can say for your brother Tony. He's put on a few party manners

27

for me, hasn't he? But they're wearing off now. Soon he'll be making faces behind my back and imitating my funny little ways.'

The twins said nothing. They knew quite well that was exactly what Tony would do. He would make all the boys at school scream with laughter when he imitated his Great-Aunt Grace. When Tony was funny he was very, very funny. But he was sometimes funny about the wrong things.

It was easy to be funny about Great-Aunt Grace. Very easy. She had so many strange little ways. She always had a hairpin or two falling out and she was always patting her hair to find these, and putting them back safely. She left her handkerchief behind her and was always going back for it, saying, 'Dear, dear, my memory! Where have I put my hanky this time?'

She couldn't bear any crumb, hair or fleck of dust on her dress, and she was always flicking away real or imaginary ones with her finger and thumb. Tony could imitate all these things to perfection, and even Lizzie had to laugh when he began. To see Tony patting about for falling hairpins in his short dark hair, suddenly pretending to find one and push it back, beaming, was too much for any of the children. But it was dreadful when he began to do it just behind Aunt Grace.

Delia was a terrible giggler when once she

began. She would start to giggle and that would set the others off, too. Mrs Farrell would look up in surprise and wonder what there was that was so funny in Tony patting his head. But Aunt Grace knew. She didn't think it was funny. She thought it was bad manners and she was hurt.

'Do shut up, Tony, doing those things in front of Aunt Grace herself,' said Lizzie. 'Honestly, it's awful of you.'

'You laughed like anything,' said Tony. 'Humbug!'

'I know I did – because I simply couldn't help it,' said Lizzie. 'But I hated myself for laughing. Don't do it, Tony.'

'Little goody-goody,' said Tony. He picked up a pair of his mother's glasses and put them on, peering through them just like Lizzie. He fastened a piece of string round his front teeth,

and began to look coy and shy, trying to squeeze himself into a corner. Pam roared.

'Oh, Tony – you look just like old Lizzie does! You're a scream. Lizzie, that's how you behave, exactly!' Lizzie looked and went red. Yes, she did behave like that – she did try to fade away into corners. But how silly it looked when Tony imitated her, and anyhow she couldn't help wearing glasses and a wire round her teeth!

'Don't,' she said. 'You're unkind, Tony. You're always unkind. You're so good-looking and clever that you don't know what it's like not to be – you shouldn't make fun of people who are not.'

'Our Liz!' said Tony, going all serious again and pretending to be Lizzie fussing round Aunt Grace. 'Our ministering angel! Aunt Grace, can I get you a cushion? Oh no, Aunt Grace, I don't mind fetching your hanky. I've nothing else to do! Shall I give Sukie some water?'

Tears came into Lizzie's eyes. 'You're *mean*!' she cried. 'I don't want to be like that. I'd like to be – to be pretty like Pam. I hate being called Lizzie when my name is Elizabeth. Why can't you call me Elizabeth? I've asked you all to heaps of times. Who can help being plain and gawky if they're called Lizzie?'

'Don't blame it on your name,' said Pam, spitefully. 'You'd be just as awful if we called you Elizabeth. Elizabeth Farrell – Lizzie Farrell – you're just the same person, whatever we call you.'

'Elizabeth Farrell – it's a nice name,' said Lizzie. 'I'd like to be called that. I would feel different, whatever you say.'

'If you were a writer or an actress you could change your name to Elizabeth at once, if you wanted to,' said Delia's clear voice.

When she was alone again, Lizzie sat and thought about it. One day she would change her name to Elizabeth. She couldn't be an actress because she wasn't a bit of good at acting. But she might be a writer, perhaps.

But that's years and years ahead, she thought and looked sadly out of the window. Years and years. And now I'm growing into a Lizzie person. I shan't be able to change into an Elizabeth when I really get the chance!

Aunt Grace came into the room to look for her handkerchief. 'A penny for your thoughts, Lizzie,' she said.

'Oh, well – they're not worth a penny!' said Lizzie. 'I was just wishing something, that's all.'

'I love to know what people are wishing,' said Aunt Grace. 'Go on, child, tell me!'

'It wasn't anything much,' said Lizzie. 'I was just wishing I was old enough to *be* something – a writer, for instance – and call myself Elizabeth

Farrell instead of Lizzie. I hate being called Lizzie. Elizabeth is such a lovely name. I'm sure I shouldn't feel so silly and shy and awkward if I was called Elizabeth.'

'Well, I will call you Elizabeth, if you like,' said Aunt Grace, at once.

'Oh *no*,' said Lizzie, hastily. 'The others would laugh like anything. But wouldn't it be nice to see a book I had written, with my name across it – Elizabeth Farrell – just like that. I'd know I was somebody then, instead of the stupidest person in my family.'

'I don't see any reason at all why you shouldn't write a book some day,' said Aunt Grace. 'You always write me extremely good letters. Why don't you write a story and sign it Elizabeth Farrell, just to see what it feels like?'

'Oh, I couldn't write a story!' said Lizzie, laughing. 'I can write essays for school and letters, of course, but you have to be awfully clever to write a story, don't you?'

'Well, perhaps you are awfully clever and we don't know it!' said Aunt Grace. 'I heard you telling the twins the other day about somebody's cats. It sounded most amusing to me. Why don't you write the story of the cats?'

'Oh, I couldn't,' said Lizzie, shying away at the thought. 'I'm not clever enough. Really I'm not.'

'How do you know?' cried Aunt Grace, suddenly exasperated. 'How do you know till you try? Bless the child, she's scared of everything, even herself! Elizabeth Farrell, if you want to stop being Lizzie, take hold of yourself and *do* something. Always running away from things and people! Elizabeth would never do that. No. Elizabeth Farrell would be full of dignity and charm, she'd hold her own with anyone, she'd be worthwhile. Now, where did I put my handkerchief?'

Aunt Grace found her handkerchief and then, hearing Sukie the parrot squawking, went off to see what was the matter. Lizzie stared out of the window again. A little core of excitement began to grow in her mind.

'"The Thirteen Cats" by Elizabeth Farrell,' she said, under her breath. '"Tales of my Great-Great-Granny" by Elizabeth Farrell. "Fairytales from Austria" by Elizabeth Farrell. Doesn't it sound lovely? Lizzie might not be able to do things like that but Elizabeth could. I shall be Elizabeth part of the time and write the stories I've heard – and even ones I haven't heard, ones I can make up myself. Elizabeth Farrell can do anything!'

She stood up, her face glowing. She felt that she must begin that very instant. Then she heard Tony's voice in the distance. How he would laugh if he knew! How they would all laugh. To them she was plain, gawky Lizzie, with her spectacles and the wire across her front teeth, spoiling her smile – they would never admit she was Elizabeth Farrell, writer of tales!

Well, I'll do it in secret then, thought Lizzie. I shan't tell anyone. Why didn't I think of it before? I'll write the first story, and when I've finished I'll sign my name at the end – Elizabeth Farrell. And nobody, nobody will ever know!

But it wasn't so easy to write a story after all. To begin with, it had to be done in secret, and it was difficult to do anything really privately in the House at the Corner. People always seemed to be rushing in and out of everybody else's rooms. Lizzie had never minded before, and she got very cross about it now.

First her mother would come and open the door. 'Oh, Lizzie dear, are you there? It's such a nice afternoon, don't sit indoors. Come along out.'

Or the twins would come bursting in. 'Oh, sorry, Liz. Could you lend us a copying-ink pencil? We want to write some garden labels.'

Or Greta the housekeeper would come bustling in, singing her usual little Viennese air, flapping a duster as she came. 'Oh Miss Lizzie, I distairb you! I go very soon. What are you doing here, so lonely and quiet?'

Or Tony would barge in, whistling, and then stop in surprise. 'Hello, are you here? I keep forgetting you're in the spare room now instead of in your own room. I want something out of the cupboard.'

'I wish you'd let me have a little peace and quiet!' Lizzie would say at last, getting tired of quickly covering up her writing. 'Anyone would think this was the playroom or something!'

'What do you want peace and quiet for?' demanded Tony. 'Got a secret? Ha, Lizzie's got a secret!'

'Shut up, Tony,' Lizzie would say. 'As if anyone could have secrets in this house!'

But in spite of all the interruptions and disturbances Lizzie did at last manage to finish writing her first story. There it was, in her desk, 'The Thirteen Cats. A Story for Children, by Elizabeth Farrell'. She signed her name at the end, proudly and slowly.

Elizabeth Farrell. It looked fine. And, as she signed it, Lizzie felt changed. She had done something. She had written a good story, a story no one else had written. She could be Elizabeth as much as Lizzie. In fact Elizabeth was a much finer person than Lizzie – nicer altogether, Lizzie thought. She longed to show her story to somebody.

But not to Tony or the others, she thought. I simply couldn't bear them to laugh at it – and they would. They've always made fun of me. They can't help it now. Whatever I do will be funny to them. I can never be Elizabeth Farrell to them. But I will be to myself.

She took off her glasses and the wire from her front teeth. She pushed back her heavy dark hair and looked at herself in the glass. Her eyes shone because she was happy over her story. Her cheeks were red. She looked quite different already, she thought – not pretty, like Pam, but not plain or homely any more.

'That's Elizabeth in the mirror now,' she said to herself. 'I can always be Elizabeth when I want to. And I shan't tell anyone, then nobody can laugh and spoil it all!'

4

Back at School Again

The summer term began. All the children went back to school. Pam was in the highest form, eager to take her scholarship exam and win it, and to go to college the next term.

'Of course, it doesn't really matter if I win it, or not,' she told Jean, her best friend. 'I'm going to college anyhow. But I might as well win it!'

'Nobody stands a chance against you,' said Jean. 'You've always been top of your form. But it's open to other schools as well, you know, and they say that Summerdene School has got some good brains this year.'

'I can win it standing on my head!' said Pam. 'I wish you were going to college too, Jean. Surely you don't *want* to go in for Domestic Science?'

'Well, I do,' said Jean. 'I haven't any longings to go into an office and answer the telephone all day long, or write letters dictated to me, or add up rows of figures. I want to be the centre of a home, like women used to be.'

Pam stared at her. 'Whatever do you mean?' she said.

'Yes,' said Jean, in an obstinate voice. 'When I look at my mother and see how happy she is in her own home, and how we all love to be there, and when I see all the things she knows how to do so well, I just want to be like her, that's all. I want a home of my own, and to be in it, to be the centre of everything, to make jam for my family, and pickles, and bottle fruit – I want my children to eat the things I've made myself. I want to hear them say, like we say to my mother, "Mums, this is the best strawberry jam I've ever tasted." Or, "Mummy, you're a darling to ice my birthday cake so beautifully." Well, I can learn all that kind of thing at a Domestic Science course, and that's why I want to go.'

This was a very long speech for Jean to make. Pam was astonished.

'You're mad,' she said at last. 'Fancy wanting to get back into your home when you've got the chance to get out of it! Everyone knows that housework and cooking are drudgery.'

'They're not, if you do them well, and know how to do them,' said Jean. 'You've never polished a fine oak table and been pleased to see how it shines. Well, I have. And you've never gathered redcurrants out of your own garden and made them into redcurrant jelly for your brothers to eat in the winter – you don't know how good it is to see people enjoying what you've made for them. It's a lovely happy feeling, Pam. I'd rather be the centre of a home, a real home like that, than a little unknown person in somebody's office, with only a typewriter and a telephone to mess about with.'

'I've never heard you make such long speeches!' said Pam. 'You sound like my great-aunt Grace. She is always talking like that, nagging at me because I don't know even how to cook an egg! You're old-fashioned.'

'No, I'm not,' said Jean. 'I'm new-fashioned. I don't want to rush away from my home as girls have been doing for years – I want to be the centre of it, the star of it, making it lovely, filling its shelves with jams and bottles and pickles and eggs – always having something different to do all the year round, not the same old routine of a musty little office. You're the old-fashioned one!'

Jean was so heated that Pam was surprised. 'We're not quarrelling, are we, Jean?' she said. 'You've never said so much before.'

'No. You thought it was a waste of my brains to go and take a thoroughly good Domestic Science course, and learn how to run what all families long for and very few get – a really good home!' said Jean. 'So I never said much. I've been talking to my mother though, and I know that what I'm doing is right – right for me, anyway!'

'Well, don't let's discuss it any more,' said Pam with a laugh, slipping her arm through Jean's. 'You and my sister Lizzie would get on well together. Lizzie's always rushing round the house too – poor plain Lizzie, there's nothing much else she'll be able to do!'

'I always thought Lizzie was much brainier than you make out,' said Jean. 'I heard one of the mistresses discussing her essays once, and she said they were the finest in the school.'

'Well, writing good essays won't get Lizzie a good job once she's left school,' said Pam. 'It won't be worth while sending her to college. She hasn't enough brains.'

Pam felt a bit ruffled as she left Jean to go to her class. Jean had always agreed with her in everything before. She thought perhaps it was Jean's mother that had upset her ideas. Pam didn't like Mrs Simpson. Mrs Simpson didn't laugh and think it was funny when Pam said she couldn't cook an egg. All she said was, 'Well, it would do you good to learn, my dear. You'll only be half a woman if you miss out things like that.'

Pam tossed back her pretty fair hair. She would show Mrs Simpson how smart she was! She would win that scholarship easily, with flying colours, top of the list – she would go to college and do really brilliantly. She would take a marvellous job, and earn a lot of money – she would . . .

'Pamela, three times have I asked you to bring me your book,' complained Mam'selle. 'But always you look out of the window and you smile and smile. There is no one to smile at there. What is the matter with you?'

Pamela blushed and took up her book. Soon she wouldn't have to be ticked off by Mam'selle any more. She would be living the free life of a college girl. She was just about to go dreaming again when Mam'selle drew her blue pencil right through the page she was looking at.

'Pamela Farrell, this is not the work I set you. If you have not the brains to do the work, at least try to answer the right questions!'

Pamela went back to her place, her cheeks burning. It didn't matter being ticked off by Mam'selle when you were in the third or fourth form – but in the sixth! No one else but Mam'selle would dare to do that to her. Mam'selle glanced at her and smiled to herself.

Aha! she thought. The great Pamela is annoyed. Silly, vain child. A little shock will be good for her. She is spoilt. She has everything – brains, beauty, money behind her – and yet she has no character. She would crack like a brittle stick if anything happened to her.

Not knowing anything of Mam'selle's thoughts, Pamela worked away angrily. Wait till she had got that scholarship – she'd toss her head at Mam'selle then – silly old thing, with her bun of hair and enormous glasses. In her annoyance Pamela quite forgot the endless kindnesses that Mam'selle did, the patience she had for slow pupils, the way she always gave extra

time to those who had been away ill. She had annoyed Pamela and so, for the time being at any rate, she was just a tiresome old French mistress, with a funny bun of hair and enormous glasses.

Lower down in the school, Lizzie was copying out an essay, or rather a story. To her delight a story had been set for this week's composition, and she had done her very best and enjoyed it. And she had signed it boldly – Elizabeth Farrell. It was ready to give in. Miss Lacy, her form mistress, took the work and glanced at it. She noticed the signature at the end.

'Ah – you're going to drop the name of Lizzie and use Elizabeth,' she said approvingly. 'Quite right. It's a pity you've always been called Lizzie – it will be so difficult for you to change it if you want to. But perhaps you don't want to? Lizzie doesn't really suit you.'

'Oh, I do want to,' said Lizzie, earnestly. 'But everyone would laugh if I asked them to call me something different, and it would be very difficult for them to remember, anyhow. I'm afraid I'll have to put up with it now!'

'Yes, I suppose you will,' said Miss Lacy. 'My own name is Margaret, but people have called me Daisy as long as I can remember, and I suppose they always will! I'm not a bit like a daisy, either.'

She wasn't. Margaret would have suited her well. Lizzie sighed. Names shouldn't matter, but they did. She felt so different when she was Elizabeth!

Lower down the school still was Delia, in the second form. But she was not doing any lessons. It was the hour set aside for working in the school garden, and Delia was out there, taking charge! Miss Root, the teacher in charge, was quite willing. Delia knew far more about gardening than Miss Root did! In fact, thought Miss Root, it was quite amazing what she knew, and what she did.

She had taught the class how to double-dig. She had gone to the seed merchant with her brother, David, and had ordered all the right seeds. She had measured and marked the dug ground for the crops. She was, in fact, a perfect godsend to Miss Root, who usually had to go and consult the school gardener, Tapp – and Tapp was a surly, bad-tempered fellow, not at all helpful, and quite likely to give poor Miss Root bad advice, just out of spite.

'We'll have the first row of peas here,' said Delia, in her clear voice. 'And we'll have the lettuces there. And we must watch the broad beans for black fly. Tessie, you can be responsible for that.'

Tessie's eyes popped. 'Black fly? What's black

fly?' she said. 'You do give me awful things to do, Delia.'

'Don't be silly,' said Delia. 'It's the very easiest thing I can think of, for somebody who doesn't know a spade from a rake!'

She set two children to wheel away rubbish. She told Hilary to weed the path. Miss Root sat on a barrow and watched. Really, Delia was a marvel at gardening – and at all kinds of nature too. There wasn't a weed she didn't know. She knew all the birds and could even tell them by their songs. Miss Root felt quite small when she thought of all that Delia knew and she didn't.

'Miss Root,' said Delia, coming up to her. 'You haven't anything to do, have you? Well, you might clear away those . . .'

But that was too much for Miss Root. She rose up with dignity. 'Delia, *I* am in charge here,' she said. 'Just get on with your work, please. Really, you Farrells think too much of yourselves at times!'

5

Michael has an Idea

Aunt Grace enjoyed being at the House at the Corner. It was a lively house, with something always going on. Mr Farrell was a surgeon, and went off every day to his hospital and private patients. He drove off in his big car, a quiet, kindly-faced man, absorbed in his work of bringing health and happiness back to as many people as he could.

He was Aunt Grace's nephew, and she loved him and was proud of him. She had helped him when he was young and had not had much money to make his way, and he loved the old lady and always made her welcome.

'You may laugh at Aunt Grace,' he sometimes said to his wife, when she grumbled at having to have the old lady to stay, 'and you may think she's a tiresome nuisance, with her parrot and her fussy ways and sharp tongue – but she's got a heart of gold and I shall never forget how kind and generous she was to me when I was struggling to get on in my work!'

'I wish her heart of gold would show a bit more, then,' said Mrs Farrell. 'She's really too sharp-tongued with Pam for anything! Pam's almost grown up now and she won't stand being ticked off like a child. And Aunt Grace isn't above telling me a few things too!'

John Farrell smiled at his pretty, indignant wife. She was so like Pam, sweet to look at, quick in her ways, but she, too, found it difficult to be tidy and responsible and methodical. She was quite lost if her husband ever went away for a while and left her to manage things. I've spoilt her, thought her husband. And now she's spoiling Pam. But Lucy isn't selfish like Pam, thank goodness. Pam is getting hard and wilful. And what shall I do with that monkey of a Tony? I'll give him a chance to turn over a new leaf when he goes into a higher form. If he doesn't I shall have to have a talk with the headmaster.

Then he began to think about his work again. He loved every minute of it. He had hoped that Tony might like to be a doctor or a surgeon too, but he saw that the boy was far too irresponsible ever to be trusted with people's lives. Lizzie now; if she had been a boy – but she wasn't. He looked at his watch. Time for him to go to the hospital – ah, there was Aunt Grace, putting Sukie's cage into the sun.

'Hello, Aunt Grace,' he said, and went out to talk to her for a minute. 'I hope you and Sukie are happy here.'

'We are,' said Aunt Grace, smiling up at her tall, dark-haired nephew. Little bits of grey showed at his temples now, and it suited him, she thought. That was one of the best things she had ever done in her life – helping John when he was young! She was proud of him and fond of him.

'There's always something going on here,' said Aunt Grace, filling Sukie's pan with water. 'Pam playing the piano, Tony making somebody laugh, Lizzie doing the flowers, the twins shouting about the garden, Greta singing one of her Austrian songs, the hens cackling because they had laid eggs, the bees buzzing in and out of the hives in the garden, Lucy calling somebody, you driving up in your car . . . oh, it's a lively house, and I'm very happy here.'

'Good,' said her nephew and he gave his old aunt a quick squeeze. 'Well, old lady, you helped to make it all, you know: if you hadn't helped me as you did, I couldn't have become a busy surgeon, I couldn't have married Lucy and bought back our old house, the children wouldn't be here, it's all your doing, really!'

Aunt Grace turned away to hide the sudden tears that came to her eyes. All her doing! Well, that was something, anyway. She had made so many silly mistakes in her life, it was good to hear of something worthwhile she had done.

Dear old John – he knew the meaning of gratitude, and so few people did.

'I'm glad you're doing well, John,' she said, giving Sukie a good supply of the sunflower seeds she loved. 'Making enough money to keep your large family happy and well provided for! Pam going to college, and Tony too later on, I suppose and . . .'

'John, haven't you gone yet?' cried Mrs Farrell, from the window. 'It's past ten o'clock. You'll be late!'

'So I shall,' said Mr Farrell, and smiled at Aunt Grace. 'Keeping me talking here! See you at lunch-time!'

Off he went in his big car. The sun shone down warmly. The bees buzzed in and out of the hives that old Frost kept at the bottom of the garden. He had shown the twins the insides, and had taught them all he knew about bees. They had been stung, but didn't seem to mind. They knew all about the hens too, and had wanted to keep ducks as well, if Frost would only dig a small pond for them.

'No, really, hens are quite enough,' their mother said. 'Why you want to mess about with hens and ducks and bees I can't imagine! Still, it keeps you out of mischief, I suppose.'

The twins were sad at having to go to different schools. If only they could go to a school that took both boys and girls! But there wasn't one in Rivers-End, their town.

Then, one day when they had gone to see their great friend, Michael Best, the son of the Rector, he had told them something that excited them very much.

'Why don't you ask your father if you can go to boarding-school?' he said. 'There are co-ed schools, you know, that take both boys and girls together – fine for twins like you!'

'Co-ed – whatever does that mean?' asked Delia. 'What a funny name.'

'It means co-educational, boys and girls together being educated,' explained Michael. 'But perhaps your parents don't believe in boarding-school?'

'I don't know about that,' said Delia. 'Pam and Lizzie never wanted to go, and Mummy always says she couldn't bear to let Tony leave her even for a week. But I'd love to go with David – we shouldn't feel a bit lost or lonely there if we had each other – but I'd want to go to a school that let us keep pets and things, and gave us a garden of our own.'

'You want to go to Whyteleafe School then!' said Michael. 'That's a fine school; you have your own pets there, they keep hens and ducks and bees and the children manage the school garden themselves. They grow all their own vegetables and fruit and flowers. There are horses to ride too, but the children look after them themselves.'

David and Delia began to glow. This sounded perfectly wonderful! 'Michael! If only we could go! We're so tired of always being "the babies" at home, and of getting in Tony's way, or Pam's. But do they do lessons at this school? Daddy wouldn't let us go if they didn't.'

'Idiot! Of course they do!' said Michael, laughing. 'They work very hard. And they have a sort of School Parliament, you know – have a meeting every week, and make their own rules, and mete out their own punishments and rewards. It's jolly sensible. You'd like it.'

David and Delia looked at one another. Each thought the same. 'We'll ask Daddy about it at once!'

'We'd better get the – the – what-do-you-call-it – paper about the school,' said David.

'The prospectus,' said Michael. 'Yes, you get that, and read up all about the school and find out how much the fees are and everything. Then you'll be ready to talk it over with your father and mother – nothing like having everything at your finger-tips! I'll write and get the prospectus for you if you like. Of course, the school may be too expensive. Your father's got a lot of you to educate, you know!'

'Yes. Well, we won't ask to go if it's too expensive,' said Delia. 'But we could find out. Thanks awfully, Michael. You really are a fine friend to have!'

Michael grinned. He was fifteen, much older than the twins, but he thought a lot of them. He was the only child of the Rector, and a very fine boy. In the holidays he held a Sunday Class for anyone who liked to come, and the twins went each Sunday.

Michael had a serious side to him and a jolly side too. He meant to go into the Church like his father when he was older. 'You see, I'm a bit like your father,' he explained to the twins. 'He can't be happy unless he is curing diseased and deformed bodies, and bringing back health and happiness to them. Well, I shan't be happy unless I can cure diseased and deformed minds. Your father's a doctor who mends bodies. I shall be a doctor who mends souls.'

'I shall come to you if ever my soul wants mending,' promised Delia, solemnly. 'How will you mend it? How do souls get mended?'

'I shouldn't think your soul will give you much trouble, Delia,' said Michael, looking down at the serious, kind little face turned up to him. 'Not if you go on as you have begun, anyway. Now, let's go exploring, shall we, and see how many birds we can spot today.'

Michael was as keen on nature as the twins were. No one else in Rivers-End knew as much as Michael and the twins about birds and flowers and animals. When the twins disappeared for whole days in the holidays, their mother always knew where they were – at the Rectory with Michael, or roaming the woods and hills with him – having tea with Mrs Best, the Rector's wife, or looking through the Rector's old books.

'They're not a bit like ordinary children,' she complained to Aunt Grace. 'They don't play the ordinary games, or ask their friends here to play, they're always studying some horrid creature or other – a hedgehog or a mole, or some caterpillar or worm! And whenever I ask them about what they are doing, they just shut up and look obstinate. Really, they might hardly belong to the family at all!'

'Lucy, they're not likely to tell you much about their beloved "creatures" if you think those creatures horrid and disgusting,' said Aunt Grace, her knitting needles going in and out with vigour. 'They know you disapprove of their liking for out-of-doors things, so naturally they won't tell you anything. Also, they are twins, and have each other as constant companions; they don't need other children as Tony and Pam do.'

Tony was there, listening. 'I can't think why the twins are so friendly with that priggish Best boy,' he said. 'Going to his Sunday Class, and half living at the Rectory in the hols! They'll be turning into pious little prigs themselves next.'

'Oh, no they won't,' said Aunt Grace, who was fond of the twins and amused with their determined, solemn ways. 'Just because they are really serious about the things they do doesn't mean they will be prigs. It would do you good, Tony, to be serious about something occasionally – your work for instance! People who can never take anything seriously aren't much good in the world.'

'Oh, Tony will work hard as soon as he gets out of that silly Mr Blinky's class,' said Mrs Farrell, anxious to defend Tony. 'You can't blame a high-spirited boy for making fun of a master who doesn't know how to keep order in his class.'

'Well, I do blame him,' said Aunt Grace,

unable to keep her tongue still once she had started. 'You'll be sorry, Lucy, if you let him behave like this at his age! It will be too late, when he does make up his mind to use his brains in the proper way!'

'Aunt Grace, I can use my brains better than any boy in my class if I want to,' said Tony, stung by the outspoken things Aunt Grace was saying. 'And I'd rather be myself than a prig like Michael Best – running a Sunday Class and being Scoutmaster, and organising sports for the village boys. Pooh!'

'I'm not going to argue with a small boy like you, Tony,' said Aunt Grace, trying hard to keep her temper. 'But I should just like you to know that Michael Best has passed all his exams with top marks, he is captain of his games at school and that he won the scholarship he wanted with

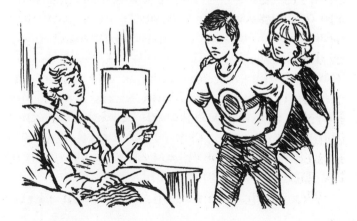

higher marks than any boy has ever won! How you can call a boy like that a prig beats me! It would be a good thing if you went and helped him with the Scouts in the village. I think . . .'

But Tony was gone, banging the door rudely behind him. Mrs Farrell looked upset. Aunt Grace knitted furiously, feeling angry with herself for losing her temper.

'I'm sorry, Lucy,' she said at last. 'Sorry for upsetting you, I mean. Perhaps you are right, Tony will make a great effort when he goes into a higher form, and will show us all what he can really do when he tries.'

'I'm sure he will,' said Mrs Farrell, earnestly. 'Look at Pam, always top of her form. And Tony has just as good brains, you know. All the same I think you're right about Michael Best, he isn't a prig. He's just a – a . . .'

'A fine natural boy, using his strength of mind and body to do his best in every way,' said Aunt Grace. 'And he's the best friend those twins of yours could have! It's a pity he isn't Tony's friend as well.'

No more was said. Aunt Grace forgot her burst of temper. Mrs Farrell thought of something else. Only Tony remembered and was angry. How dare Aunt Grace find fault with him like that? Horrid, interfering old woman!

6

A Family Talk

Michael wrote for the prospectus for Whyteleafe School. It came and he gave it to the twins. They studied it with delight. It was just exactly the school!

'And we'd be together all day,' said Delia. 'David, let's ask Daddy and Mummy tonight.'

So, when the family was gathered together for a while after the evening meal, the twins sprang their idea on their astonished parents.

'Daddy, could you afford to send us to a boarding-school?' asked Delia, suddenly. Her father looked up in surprise.

'Why do you ask that?' he said. 'Yes, of course I could. But Pam and Lizzie have never wanted to go, and your mother wouldn't let Tony leave home. What's the idea?'

David produced the prospectus. 'We'd very much like to go to this school, if you could afford it, Daddy,' he said. 'The main reason, of course, is that we're twins, and we don't like going to different schools. And then we're really interested in nature and gardening and animals and things like that – and this school really does go in for all those.'

Their mother had been listening in complete amazement. Well! This was the first she had heard of the idea! Those twins! Nobody ever knew what they were thinking. She felt a little annoyed.

'What's this school?' she asked. 'Really, twins, you seem to decide everything for yourselves without even consulting us! Bringing the prospectus and everything!'

'Well, Mummy, we thought it would be a help if we found out everything first,' said Delia. 'Michael Best told us about the school – he got the prospectus for us too.'

There was a snort from Tony. 'He would! Interfering prig! Mum, it's awful sauce on his part, putting the twins up to this.'

'I should have thought you would have been glad to be rid of us, Tony,' said David. 'We're always in your way. You're always calling us "the babies" and ordering us out of your sight.'

Mrs Farrell looked upset. 'David! Don't say things like that. No one would be glad to be rid of you. You make us sound a horrid family – instead of a – of a most united one.'

Delia had a very honest, straight-thinking mind, and she had not learned to keep her thoughts to herself. So she spoke out in her clear voice and gave everyone quite a shock.

'Oh, Mummy, we're not really very united, are we? Lizzie's one on her own, isn't she? And Tony and Pam haven't much use for us, so we're on our own too. Pam only thinks of school and going to college, she doesn't help you at all even when you want her to – she doesn't really *belong* to the family. And . . .'

There was an indignant cry from Pam. 'Mother! Are you going to let Delia talk like that? How dare she!'

Mr Farrell had been listening in silence. Now he spoke in his calm, kindly voice, and nobody dared to interrupt.

'Aren't we a united family? I had always thought we were and I'm sure Mother thought so too. But I'm not so sure that little Delia isn't right! Pam does only think of herself and going off to college now, Lizzie's so shy that she hardly lets us know her – our own fault, I expect, for teasing her so much, and always pushing her into the background and letting her do the jobs nobody else will do . . .'

'Like meeting me at the station,' put in Aunt Grace, to everyone's horror.

'Perhaps,' said Mr Farrell, gravely. 'I don't know. And there's Tony, only happy if he's attracting attention and making others laugh, and now the twins want to go off to boarding-school!'

'John! Why are you talking like this?' cried Mrs Farrell, quite frightened. 'Aren't you proud of our little family? We *are* a united family, I don't care what you say. And I won't let the twins go to boarding-school. They're the babies and they're too young to go. I should miss them so.'

Delia looked in despair at David. Of course, Mummy would say a thing like that! Now Daddy would say no at once.

But he didn't. He looked across at Aunt Grace who sat knitting busily by the window, hearing everything but saying not a word.

'Aunt Grace! You haven't said a word. What do you think about all this?'

'I don't think I want to interfere,' said Aunt Grace, afraid that she might say more than she should.

'I'm not asking you to interfere,' said Mr Farrell. 'I'm asking you what you think about it all. You could probably help us.'

Aunt Grace put down her knitting and looked round. She saw Pam's sulky face, and Tony's cross one. She saw Lizzie's homely face, shy and scared at the sudden upset. She saw the twins' earnest faces, so very alike, looking disappointed and miserable.

'Delia's right, you know,' said Aunt Grace. 'You're not really a united family, you don't

belong together, somehow. I think perhaps
Lizzie's the only one who belongs to all of you,
but she's so scared of things you don't know it!'

'Why should families be united, as you call
it?' said Pam, scornfully. 'It doesn't matter a
scrap if they are or not!'

'Oh yes it does,' said Aunt Grace. 'What do
you find in a really united family? You find love
and comradeship, understanding and com-
passion, unselfishness and gentleness with one
another – you learn things there that will last you
well all your life long. It's the best grounding for
a good, worthwhile life that there is anywhere.

Think of families you know that are not united – quarrelling, selfish, mean, disloyal, nagging, hating – what a way to start out in life!'

The children all thought of families they knew. Mrs Rowley's family. She had a nagging tongue and had brought up a spiteful, disloyal trio of girls. Mrs Thomas's family: she was always out and her home wasn't a home, just a place where the children came in and out as they pleased, and nobody knew where anyone else was or what they were doing. Mrs Kennard's family: Mrs Kennard, lazy and irresponsible, letting her three children grow up untrustworthy, untruthful, telling tales of one another, and taking each other's things.

'We're not like the Kennards or the Rowleys!' burst out Lizzie. 'We're not! We do stick up for one another, and help one another.'

'You do, Lizzie,' said Delia. 'But nobody else does. Look how David and I want to go to boarding-school, just because we're twins and hate being apart – but nobody sticks up for us and understands that. Even Mummy doesn't. She just thinks she will miss us and doesn't at all think of how we miss one another, David and I. You see, if we were a proper united family, you'd all understand how we felt and you'd back us up.'

'Mother! How can you let Delia be so smug

and – and – so cheeky?' cried Pam, angry to think that everyone was listening so seriously to her 'baby' sister. 'She wants a good spanking.'

'No, she doesn't,' said her father. 'She's quite right in what she says. But suppose, Delia, I couldn't really afford to send you both to this school? It's quite expensive.'

'Oh, Daddy, if it's too much money we wouldn't dream of going,' said Delia, earnestly, and David nodded. 'We wouldn't really. But we don't know much about money, so we couldn't tell. We wouldn't like anyone to have to go short of anything because of us.'

'There you are!' said Aunt Grace, in a triumphant voice. 'There's a real bit of family unselfishness for you! Delia and David want something badly – but not at the expense of anyone else's happiness. They've got the right idea, young as they are. They deserve to get what they want, that's what *I* say!'

'You're right,' said Mr Farrell, and he smiled at the twins. 'They deserve it, and I don't see why they shouldn't have it if Lucy agrees. I can afford it. I think it would be a great happiness to them to be together at this school – which, I must say, seems to be a very sound and sensible one.'

The twins looked dumbfounded. They stared at one another and then round at everyone else.

Then they looked at their mother. She nodded at them, her eyes full of tears, trying to smile.

'Yes, I'll let you go, dears,' she said. 'I didn't think you minded so much. I can't remember that you aren't babies any more. You'll be happy at boarding-school, and you'll always be together then. I'll go to your head teachers myself tomorrow and give notice for you to leave at the end of this term. You shall go to Whyteleafe in September.'

The twins flung themselves on their mother, too delighted for words. She hugged them.

'We'll look at the school list of clothes and see what you must get,' she said, 'and we'll see what pets you can have. You'll be so happy!'

'You're a darling, Mummy!' said Delia. 'I never really thought you'd let us go. You do know it's not because we don't like home, don't you? You do know it's really mostly because we want to be together, David and I?'

Pam slipped out of the room, her face sulky. 'Spoiling those two brats!' she whispered to herself. 'Anyway, they'll be a good riddance! Daddy oughtn't to have given in like that, though. I suppose he thinks he can afford to send them away because I shall win that scholarship and he won't have to pay my college fees! Lucky for Delia and David that they've got a clever sister!'

She bumped into Greta, who was looking cross. 'Ah, Pamela,' she began. 'Twice today have I tidied your room and I have so much to do. Now a third time it is all upset, with your dresses on the floor and your books all over the place. I have no time to tidy it. This time you must tidy it yourself.'

'Well, I shan't,' said Pam, rudely. 'It's your job to do that. I'm going out!'

Greta flared up, but before she could say anything Pam had gone. Grumbling to herself Greta went into the kitchen.

'One day I shall pack and go if that girl does

not treat me properly!' she said, and banged the kettle down on the stove. 'That Tony too, with his silly jokes and tricks, one day I shall give him an ear-box. And that parrot with its "squook, squook!"'

The twins came running out to her. 'Greta, Greta! We're going to boarding-school in September – think of that – *together*! We're going together!'

Hot-tempered Greta forgot her rage and beamed at the two children. 'Ah, how nice for you!' she said. 'I too had a twin once, and I know how bad it is to part. You shall have a jam tart new from the oven to show how I am glad.'

'Greta, you might be one of the family, the way you are glad or sad with us,' said Delia, munching her jam tart. 'I do like you.'

'Ah, one of the family!' said Greta, with one of her enormous, exaggerated sighs. 'Once I was also one of the family. Now I am alone and my family is dead. It is a good thing to have a family, I tell you. I have none.'

'Well, you must share ours,' said Delia, generously. 'We'd like you to, wouldn't we, David?' And David, his mouth full of warm jam tart, nodded vigorously.

7

The Farrell Family are Busy

May came in and the sun grew warmer. The bees in the hives at House at the Corner buzzed busily. Late daffodils and early tulips blossomed in the garden there. Sukie the parrot spent the whole day out in the sun and grew very talkative indeed.

The twins taught her some more sayings. She was a clever, imitative bird, and soon picked up anything if it was said to her often enough.

'Where's my hanky?' she suddenly began to say, over and over again. Aunt Grace was indignant.

'Don't you teach Sukie to make fun of me!' she said to the twins.

But it was not Delia nor David who had taught the parrot to say that, it was Tony! And now Sukie greeted everyone with 'Where's my hanky?' and poor Aunt Grace didn't dare to say it any more. She was glad when the twins began to teach the parrot to say 'hip-hip-hooray' and wave one of her feet in the air.

Pam was happy at school that term. Her form was giving a play, and there was a beautiful princess in it. She had been chosen for the part.

'I don't think Pam ought to have such a long and exacting part, in the term when she is hoping to take her scholarship exam,' said Miss Dawes, the headmistress, to Pam's form-mistress. 'I don't see how she can cram for her exam and learn this long part too.'

'She seems to think she can,' said Miss Peters. 'She has a very fine memory, you know. She only has to look at a page and she knows it! But if you think she should take a smaller part, I will tell her.'

'I'll speak to her about it,' said Miss Dawes, and called Pam into her room. Pam's face fell when she heard her headmistress suggesting that she should have a smaller part in the play because of her scholarship work.

'But, Miss Dawes,' she said. 'I can do the exam standing on my head, I know I can! I shan't need to study very much for it.'

'You must remember that a great many very clever girls will be competing for it,' said Miss Dawes. 'And for many of them it will be the only chance of getting into college. If you failed it would make no difference to you, because your father can afford to send you anyhow.'

'I shan't fail,' said Pam, confidently. 'Don't worry, Miss Dawes. Let me take the part of the princess, it won't take very much learning really.

I promise I won't slack in my other work.'

'Very well,' said Miss Dawes. 'You are old enough to be trusted, I suppose. But please remember that we shall all be very disappointed if you don't win the scholarship!'

Pam went off happily. She told Jean about her talk with Miss Dawes and laughed about it.

'Fancy thinking that taking part in a play would stop me winning the scholarship!' she said. 'As if it could.'

'Well, it's rather a long and exciting part,' said Jean. 'And you'll get rather wrapped up in it, I expect. You'll look lovely as the princess, Pam. You look very like a princess, I always think, with your mass of golden hair and your curly eyelashes – a fairytale princess!'

Pam laughed again, pleased. Yes, she would make a fine princess. She knew it. Everyone would think she filled the part very well, and all the younger girls would sigh with pleasure when they saw her in the play. She was quite a heroine to them.

At first it was easy to cram for the exam and study her part in the play too. But it was so much more fun to spend time on the play! It was a bore to have to put it aside and take up school books.

Then, too, there were the dresses Pam had to wear for the play. There were three different ones, each prettier than the last! Pam was no good at sewing, but Jean and Lizzie were, and the two of them spent a good deal of time together, sewing for Pam. Jean began to like Lizzie very much. Once she got past Lizzie's shyness, she made her talk. Lizzie found herself longing to tell Jean about her story writing, but as it would mean begging Jean not to tell Pam, she felt she couldn't. After all, Jean was Pam's friend, and it wouldn't be fair to ask her to keep things from Pam.

The story Lizzie had written at school had been most successful. It had actually been read out to the class, and Lizzie's face had burned with pride and pleasure. But best of all was when Miss Lacy had said, at the end. 'This story was written by Elizabeth Farrell.' Not Lizzie Farrell. Elizabeth.

Since then Lizzie had written more little tales in secret. She had not attempted grown-up stories. She felt she didn't know enough to do that. But she could write stories for children. She knew exactly how to tell those, because for many years she had told Delia and David stories when they were in bed.

Once Aunt Grace had found her writing busily away all by herself in the summerhouse. 'Writing letters?' she said. 'Or stories, perhaps, Elizabeth Farrell?'

Then Lizzie had blushed and laughed. 'I'm writing a new story, one I'm making up all by myself,' she said. 'For children. I'm pretending that I'm telling it to Delia and David when they were little, so that I get the words right – not too difficult, you know.'

'I suppose I mustn't see it?' said Aunt Grace, not attempting to take up the sheets of paper. Lizzie hesitated. Suppose Aunt Grace laughed at what she had done, or over-praised her in the way grown-ups had when they thought something was rather silly but didn't like to hurt your feelings about it. That would be awful. It would spoil everything.

'Don't let me see anything if you'd rather not,' said Aunt Grace. 'I once wrote myself, you know – poetry! I fancied myself at it, but I wasn't much good. But you should be able to write well. You write such good letters.'

'You can see the story, Aunt Grace,' said Lizzie, suddenly. 'After all, you started me off! But please, please don't laugh at it!'

Aunt Grace picked up the first sheet. She read it in silence. She picked up the second and the third. Lizzie tried to go on with her writing but she couldn't. She found that she was waiting most impatiently for what Aunt Grace would say. Oh quick! she cried in her thoughts. Tell me what you think, but oh, don't say it's silly.

Aunt Grace put down the sheets and looked
at Lizzie. 'Are you sure you didn't copy this
from anywhere?' she asked.

'No. No, of course not!' said Lizzie. 'It's
all out of my own head. It comes as I write
it. Oh Aunt Grace, don't say you've read it
somewhere!'

'I haven't,' said Aunt Grace. 'I've never read a story like it anywhere.'

'Then why did you ask if I'd copied it?' cried Lizzie.

'Only because it's so very good, child,' said Aunt Grace. 'Amazingly good. Interesting and simple and really amusing. You've certainly got the gift all right.'

Lizzie felt as if she could cry with relief and happiness. She gazed at Aunt Grace, unable to speak a word. Her story was good – amazingly good, Aunt Grace said. And Aunt Grace never praised like that unless she meant it.

'Well, have you lost your tongue?' asked Aunt Grace. 'Bless the child, she's as red as a beetroot!'

Lizzie gave a gulp. 'Oh Aunt Grace, do you really think it's good? I can't tell, myself. But it's such fun writing like this. I've never enjoyed myself so much in my life.'

'That's what artists say when they paint their pictures, and composers say when they create a symphony,' said Aunt Grace. 'Those of us who have gifts are the lucky ones – if we use them properly. You certainly have a gift. You must go on and on. You will give many people great pleasure.'

'But how?' asked Lizzie. 'Nobody will read these tales – except you, perhaps. The others would laugh like anything at them.'

'There's a paper I take every week,' said Aunt Grace. 'It's called *The Quiet Magazine* and it has two pages for children in it. It has always seemed to me that the stuff they put in these pages is terrible. Now why don't you send one of your tales there? It seems to me quite good enough to be printed. Then you'd see your name in print – Elizabeth Farrell!'

Lizzie was tongue-tied again. Have a story printed – one of her own stories! That would never happen. But suppose it did? What a wonderful thing. Her eyes shone behind their spectacles as she looked at her great-aunt.

'Oh Aunt Grace! It sounds impossible but I'll try it. Can you get me the address?'

'Yes. But you'll have to type out your story before you send it,' said Aunt Grace. 'Can you type? Well, you must learn. All writers should know how to type. Saves a lot of time. You can ask your father if he'll let you teach yourself on his typewriter.'

'Don't tell anyone at all, will you, Aunt Grace?' begged Lizzie, her cheeks still burning in excitement. 'It's our secret, isn't it? Oh Aunt Grace, if I had a story printed I'd die of happiness!'

'No, you wouldn't. You'd sit down and slave away at another one,' said Aunt Grace, with a laugh. 'I'll help you to learn to use the type-writer. I know how to type but my old fingers are too stiff to use a machine now.'

So, what with Lizzie learning to type, and spending many hours with her father's type-writer, tap-tap-tapping away, and Pam learning the part in her play, parading before her long mirror as she recited her lines, and Jean coming in to fit her dresses on her, and Tony shut away in his room, making something, the children were very busy. Only the twins were not much in the house. They were out in the garden, busy there as usual, weeding, sowing, hoeing and bedding out.

Tony was busy concocting one of his practical jokes. This was his last term in Blinky's class and he meant to make the most of it. Nobody had ever dared to play tricks in Snorter's class. He was quite capable of marching the culprit off to the headmaster then and there, and demanding immediate punishment!

Old Blinky will get the surprise of his life soon! thought Tony, very busy mixing this, that and the other together. Soon a perfectly horrible smell arose.

'Want it a bit worse than that,' said Tony to himself, making a face. 'Just a bit. Phoooo! That's better! That'll make old Blinky sit up a bit. I'll make a bottle full of it, and keep my little sprayer in my pocket. Then whenever Blinky turns round to the blackboard, I'll spray a little of the mixture over his desk. What a shock he'll get when he sits down!'

The door opened and Aunt Grace looked in. 'Tony! What is the dreadful smell coming from your room?'

'Nothing, Aunt Grace,' said Tony, crossly. 'Just practising a bit of my chemistry homework, that's all.'

The door shut on Aunt Grace's annoyed face. She didn't like the tone of Tony's voice. Tony made a face at the shut door.

'Interfering old thing!' he said, in a voice that he hoped would reach his great-aunt. 'I wish you and old Blinky were in my classroom together when I play this trick. It would serve you right to get a bit of my mixture.'

8

Lizzie loses her Temper

The early summer passed on in a blaze of sunshine and blue sky. May was a beautiful month that year. Pam worked hard at the play, but did less and less studying for the scholarship. Tony waited for a chance to play his trick. He had told all his class about it, sworn them to secrecy, and was longing for the chance to try out this horrible-smelling mixture.

Lizzie was learning to type and getting on quite well. She had typed out her story as neatly as she could, but Aunt Grace had said there were too many mistakes. So she had had to try again. Now it was done, and Aunt Grace had approved.

'You can send it now,' she said. 'I've sent for my magazine, and here it is. You'll find the address on the first page. Be sure to put a stamped addressed envelope in with the story.'

'But why?' asked Lizzie, surprised. 'Oh, I see – to send it back if they don't want it. Oh, Aunt Grace, I couldn't bear it to be sent back!'

'It's a thing that most writers have to bear when they begin,' said Aunt Grace, cheerfully. 'If you are successful immediately you'll be very lucky. My word, doesn't your name look nice on the story – Elizabeth Farrell. It's a good name for a writer.'

Lizzie typed out an envelope addressed to herself and put a stamp on it. Then she typed out another envelope addressed to *The Editor, The Quiet Magazine*, and put her story into it. 'Wish me luck, Aunt Grace,' she said, in rather a trembly voice. It seemed to her to be a very daring, important thing to do, to send something she had written to the editor of a grown-up's magazine!

Aunt Grace wished her luck and took it to the post herself for Lizzie. But alas, two days later the big envelope that Lizzie had typed to herself arrived back on the front-door mat! Tony picked it up with the other letters and took it into the playroom. 'Letter for you,' he said to Lizzie with a grin. 'Addressed to "Miss Elizabeth Farrell", if you please. Who's it from?'

Up till now all the Farrell children had shared their letters, read them out to one another, and never minded anyone else seeing them. But Lizzie felt that she could not possibly say anything about this letter. She fingered it anxiously. Oh dear, oh dear, it felt thick, as if the story had been sent back already!

'Open it, silly, and see who it's from!' said Tony.

'I know who it's from,' said Lizzie. 'It's – it's nothing important.'

'Don't be so secretive, Lizzie,' said Pam, overcome with curiosity. 'Let's see what's in it.'

'No,' said Lizzie. 'I'm going to open it when I want to – not now.'

Tony snatched the letter from her and tore it open. Lizzie flew at him at once, trembling with sudden rage. Her letter – her story – her precious secret! How dare Tony do a thing like that!

Tony danced round the room, holding the long envelope above his head, tearing it open as he did so, and taking out the neatly typed story. Lizzie struggled with him and tried to get it.

'Hi! It's a story! All typed out – and my word, who do you think it's by?' yelled Tony. 'Elizabeth Farrell! Golly, she's written a silly, sloppy story and had the nerve to send it out to some paper or other. No wonder they've sent it back. Yes, look, "The Editor regrets . . . story not suitable . . . returning it with thanks"! Ha, ha, Lizzie! Did you really think you were clever enough to have a story printed? What a conceited idiot you are!'

Pam laughed too. The twins watched in astonishment, surprised at Lizzie's extraordinary behaviour. She stamped her foot, she shouted, and tears poured down her face. 'You beast, you beast, how dare you take my letter! You've spoilt everything, as I knew you would. Laugh, Pam, laugh – you're hateful, both of you, and I'll never forgive you!'

'You ought to be ashamed of behaving like that,' said Pam, coldly. 'Stop yelling and stamping, Lizzie – or shall we call you Elizabeth? Give her the letter, for goodness sake, Tony, you'll have Daddy in here wanting to know what's up. Shut up, Lizzie, do.'

Tony held out the letter and the story to poor Lizzie. The sobbing, miserable girl snatched them and tore them into little pieces. She threw them all into Tony's face.

'There you are, beast!' she sobbed. 'Take

them, take my secret. I thought I could do something and I can't. And you're glad. I hate you all!'

She rushed out of the room, almost knocking down Aunt Grace who, hearing all the noise, had come to investigate the cause. She did not stop to apologise but rushed up to her room, still sobbing.

Aunt Grace went into the playroom. 'What has happened?' she said.

'Oh, Lizzie got in a tantrum and threw things in my face,' said Tony, airily.

'But Lizzie never gets into tantrums,' said Aunt Grace, amazed. 'Whatever did you do to her?'

She saw the pieces of torn paper on the ground, bits of typing showing here and there. She stood and looked at them. Lizzie's story had come back – and somehow the others knew and had teased her and been unkind. They hadn't known what it all meant to Lizzie.

Aunt Grace glanced at Tony and Pam. Both were now feeling ashamed and were red in the face. The twins were near tears. They were fond of Lizzie and were scared to think of her so angry and unhappy.

'I don't exactly know what you've been up to, Pam and Tony,' said Aunt Grace, in a horrid sort of voice. 'But I can see it's something to be ashamed of. I am quite often ashamed of you, however, so it's nothing new.'

Leaving a dead silence behind her the old lady climbed up to Lizzie's room. The door was locked. Sobs, angry miserable sobs, came from behind it. Aunt Grace rapped smartly.

'Open the door, Lizzie. I want to talk to you,' she said.

'Please go away,' came Lizzie's trembling voice. 'I don't want anybody.'

'Open the door, please,' commanded Aunt Grace, determined to get her way. And Lizzie opened the door. Her aunt went in, sat down on the bed and pulled Lizzie to her. She let her cry for some minutes without saying anything.

'So the story came back?' she said. 'Well, who would have thought you'd be so upset about such a little thing? There are plenty of other places to send it to, only now you'll have to type it all out again because you've torn it up.'

'I – I tore it up because Tony was so beastly about it,' said Lizzie, forlornly. 'It was my secret, and he found it out and laughed at it, and jeered because the story was sent back. It was enough disappointment to have it sent back without having Tony and Pam laughing about it. I just saw red and stamped and yelled and tore it up.'

'I'm not a bit surprised at your feelings,' said Aunt Grace. 'Not a bit. Do the others good to see you can flare up now and again. Wait till you get some things accepted and printed – they'll laugh the other side of their faces then!'

'Aunt Grace, I shall never write a story again and never, never send one out anywhere,' said Lizzie, earnestly. 'Never. It was silly of me to think I was good enough.'

'Well, well, so you're just shy, scared little Lizzie Farrell after all,' said Aunt Grace, in a disappointed tone. 'And here I've been thinking of you as Elizabeth Farrell, able to do great things, and setting about them already. Lizzie's giving up at just one setback – and I had thought that Elizabeth would stand anything, so long as she knew she had the gift of writing and could work at it. But a gift is no good without character, Lizzie, no good at all. If you've not got a character strong enough to stand a defeat or disappointment now and again, you're not fit to be a great writer. Well, well, what a disappointment!'

She stood up as if to go. Lizzie looked at her in alarm. Aunt Grace's face was sad and a little scornful. Lizzie caught at her great-aunt's hand.

'Don't look like that! Don't you be scornful of me too! I know you think I'm weak and feeble – but, but . . .'

'My dear child, it rests entirely with ourselves whether we are weak and feeble or sturdy and

83

strong,' said Aunt Grace, briskly. 'I'm not talking about health, I'm talking about character, as you know. If you could take hold of this obstacle and turn it into a stepping-stone to bigger things, by saying "What's it matter? I'll try again and again – and yet again!" then you'd be all right. But you can't do it.'

'I can, I can!' said Lizzie, pulling at her aunt to stop her walking out of the door. 'Aunt Grace, don't be mean to me. I'll try again. You know I will. Give me one more chance!'

'My dear child, *I* can't give chances!' said Aunt Grace, looking down at the anxious girl. 'It is you who must give yourself chances! Just see that you take your chances, that's all! Only you can decide whether to be defeated or not.'

'Aunt Grace, I'm going straight down to the typewriter to type out that story again,' said Lizzie, screwing up her wet handkerchief and putting it into her pocket. 'As if I care whether my story's sent back the first time or not!'

She smiled a rather watery smile at her great-aunt, and got a pleased smile in return.

'Good for you, Elizabeth!' said Aunt Grace. 'We'll try somewhere else this time. I'll look out for a paper that might be suitable for your tales. Good girl! I'm proud of you!'

Lizzie went downstairs to find her father's typewriter. She sat down and began to type.

Meantime Aunt Grace was dealing with Tony, who, sulky at first, but feeling ashamed of himself, agreed in the end that he had been 'pretty beastly'.

'Then go and say so,' said Aunt Grace, firmly.

Tony was taken aback. 'What? Say I'm sorry when Lizzie flew at me like that?' he said. 'Why should I?'

'Because if you don't she may find it very difficult really to forgive you,' said Aunt Grace. 'Little things like this are what start spite and unhappiness in a family. You can put everything right now with a few words. If you don't you

85

may find you can never put things right.'

Tony put his head round the door. 'Lizzie,' he said. 'Sorry for what I did, old thing.'

Lizzie looked up, startled and pleasantly surprised. Tony disappeared – but footsteps came hurriedly after him. They were Lizzie's.

'Tony! It's all right!' she said breathlessly. 'I'm sorry too. It was all silly.'

Now it was Tony's turn to be surprised. He had expected Lizzie to be huffy and scornful with him. Instead she was her kind old self. He gave her a thump on the shoulder.

'You go on with your stories!' he said. 'I'll be the first to cheer when one's printed. See?'

Lizzie went back to the typewriter. Things seemed very different now – what a storm in a teacup! But it might have been something very much bigger – if it hadn't been for old Aunt Grace!

9

Pamela gets into Trouble

Michael Best had gone back to his school now, but the twins wrote and told him their news. He sent them back a letter which delighted them. It was good to have a friend like Michael, always helping them, sharing in their ups and downs.

Tony wanted to see the letter. He was always a little jealous of their friendship with Michael. After all, Michael was far more his age and yet he chose the twins to be his friends! Secretly, Tony admired Michael, and would have liked to do some of the things he did, such as running the scout camp in the village each summer holiday – only it was too much bother!

The twins would not let Tony see the letter. David put it firmly away in his pocket. 'No,' he said, 'you laughed at Lizzie when she got a letter. You shan't laugh at us. You always spoil things, Tony. People keep secrets from you because you laugh at them and spoil them.'

'Cheeky little beast,' said Tony. 'I've a good mind to box your ears!'

He didn't, because he had a sudden, uncomfortable feeling that David was right. He did laugh and make fun of things that other people seemed to care a lot about. 'Pooh!' said Tony to himself, 'people always make such a fuss about things. Much better to be like Pam and not take things like the scholarship seriously – make a joke of it, instead of slaving away like some kids do, making everyone miserable. And look how popular I am! Everyone starts to grin and cheer up when I come by. I wish I could get a chance to play that trick of mine. I don't dare to as long as the head wanders about, popping into classrooms unexpectedly!'

Pam was working very hard at her part in the play. It was more difficult than she had expected. The mistress who was producing the play was very anxious to make it an outstanding success, and she was driving hard all the girls who were taking part in it.

'We can't fail in any way,' she said. 'We are to give it on Speech Day, and there will be hundreds of parents and guests. I want it to be the most marvellously-acted play we have ever done. As for the dresses, they will be the best we've made!'

Pam made a most adorable princess. She had a fine, clear voice, and was very graceful. Everyone praised her and told her she should be an actress.

But Pam knew she would never make a good actress. She could learn her part well, she could

look pretty and charming, and she could do everything that Miss Romula, the drama mistress, told her to – but somehow she couldn't act naturally and convincingly. She couldn't lose herself in the part.

'She hasn't enough character herself to throw herself into other people's,' said Miss Romula. 'Things have always been too easy for Pamela. Still, she will make a fine little princess, and her pretty face and voice will make up for her second-rate acting. She is certainly working very hard to make her part a success.'

Pam was – much too hard! It began to worry her a little, and she found herself dreaming of the play at night and woke up saying her lines.

She found that it was beginning to be rather difficult to concentrate on her lessons in class. A little frown seemed always to be on her forehead. Her father noticed it.

'Pam, why do you always look so worried?' he said. 'Are you working too hard for the scholarship?'

'No, oh no,' said Pam, quite truthfully. She wasn't working hard at that at all! 'I'm just busy with the school play at the moment, that's all, Daddy. I've got the chief part, you know.'

'I think the play and the scholarship work are too much for you,' said her father, his keen doctor's eyes seeing far more than Mrs Farrell or Aunt Grace. 'Perhaps you had better drop the play. There must be others who can take your part.'

Pam stared at him in the utmost horror. What! Drop her lovely part, let someone else take it, that silly little Angela, for instance! She couldn't possibly do such a thing!

'Daddy! You don't understand,' she said, almost in tears. 'Why, my dresses are practically finished, I'm almost word-perfect – nobody else but me could possibly play that part!'

'Don't upset the child, John,' said Mrs Farrell, reproachfully. 'She couldn't possibly give up now. You've no idea how she's slaved at it.'

'That's just it,' said Mr Farrell, worried. 'She's

been doing too much. Well, I suppose it won't be long before the exam is over and the play acted; then you must slack off a bit, Pam, forget lessons for a bit and mess round the house and help your mother – that will be a change for you.' Pam scowled. Mess round the house! That was just what she didn't intend to do. Let other people make her bed and clean her room, bake the cakes and make the jam, put buttons on her blouses and do her mending! She would save her brains for other things.

'That reminds me, Pam,' said her mother, 'Greta is always complaining that you make so much work for her to do. Can't you be a little tidier in your room – clear up a bit after yourself? Greta has a lot to do here, even though she has a woman to help her in the mornings.'

'Greta's always grumbling,' said Pam, sulkily, all the prettiness gone from her face in a flash. 'I wish we could get somebody else.'

'But Greta's a darling!' said Delia, unexpectedly. 'She is, really. She's always doing things for all of us that she needn't do – isn't she, Mummy? She's quite one of the family.'

'Of course, you must put your spoke in,' said Pam, sarcastically. 'I'd like to know what Greta thinks of your two rooms, you twins, with your beastly caterpillars and smelly mice! I bet she has a few words to say about that!'

'She doesn't like them, but she's awfully nice about them,' said David. 'We know she doesn't like the mice, especially – she's scared stiff of them – so Delia and I make our own beds and tidy our own rooms as much as we can so that she doesn't have to spend too much time there.'

'You and Greta!' sneered Pam, angry to think that the twins should be bothered to tidy their own rooms when she never once thought of doing hers. 'I don't know what you can see in that silly Austrian, yelling her stupid songs all over the place, and being rude whenever she wants to.'

'That will do, Pam,' said Mrs Farrell. 'You really are very bad-tempered lately.'

'It's because she's working too hard at that play,' began Mr Farrell. 'That's just what I—'

'Oh, don't begin that all over again!' cried Pam, rudely, and went out of the room. She shut the door far too loudly. Mr Farrell went after her at once.

'Pamela! Come back. Any more behaviour of this sort and I shall go to your headmistress and ask her to let someone else take your part in the play. Come back, apologise, and shut the door quietly after you.'

Pamela stood in the hall, her heart beating angrily. How dared her father speak to her like that! She wasn't a ten-year-old, like the twins.

But the threat he had made scared her. Suppose he really did go to the head! That would be awful. She went back to the sitting-room.

'Sorry,' she mumbled, and shut the door very quietly. Then, with angry tears in her eyes she went out, scowling at the astonished Greta as she passed her. The parrot greeted her as she went out of the front porch.

'Where's your hanky? Hip-hip-hooray!' Then Sukie screeched and made Pamela jump violently.

'Hateful bird!' cried the angry girl and banged her hand on the parrot's cage, making Sukie almost fall off her perch. 'I wish you were gone – and Aunt Grace too. What beastly people live in this house!'

Lizzie and Tony had not been there when Pam had been so rude, but they heard about it from the twins. Lizzie noticed that Pam was very cool towards her father, and it distressed her. How could Pam look like that at Daddy and hardly speak to him unless she was spoken to? She was perfectly polite, but she might have been quite a stranger to him, instead of his beloved daughter. But neither Lizzie nor any of the other children dared to speak to haughty, determined Pam about it. Mr Farrell appeared not to notice it, but he was hurt and grieved.

He spoke to Aunt Grace about it. 'I expect

you've noticed that Pam won't be friends with me any more!' he said. 'But it's only because the child's overworked and upset. When this play and the scholarship exam are over she'll be her own sweet self again. So don't say anything to her, Aunt Grace, will you? It might make matters worse.'

'What Pam wants is a good spanking,' said Aunt Grace. 'You should have spanked her when she was little. Spare the rod and spoil the child! That's what you've done with Pam, John, my dear. Ah yes, I know what a pretty little thing she was, twisting you all round her little finger. Now see what you've done – made her into a hard and selfish young woman.'

'No, no,' said Mr Farrell. 'Don't be so hard on her, Aunt Grace. She's just overworked. She's behaving very badly now and perhaps I should have punished her more often when she was a naughty little girl – but she'll be sorry and as sweet as ever when this term is over.'

Aunt Grace said no more. She had never thought that Pam was sweet. She looked sweet, yes, but she wasn't. A clever brain and a pretty face were no good at all unless you had sweetness behind them. Well, something would come along to give Pam a sharp lesson one day, and the girl would just crumple up! Aunt Grace knitted vigorously, thinking hard of the Farrell family; Pam, Tony, the twins – and Lizzie.

Lizzie had written two more stories. She had typed them out carefully and correctly, for she was now very good indeed at typing. She and Aunt Grace had wondered where to send them.

'What about our local paper?' said Aunt Grace. 'You know, the *Rivers-End Weekly*? It often prints something for children. You might try there. But don't get all hot and bothered if the stories come back, Lizzie. It's what all writers have to put up with. You have to make your own name, you know, and you can only do that by trying again and again, finding out what you can write best, what people want to read, and so on. You try the *Rivers-End Weekly*.'

'I will,' said Lizzie. 'I'll send my two new stories, shall I, Aunt Grace, and the old one – the one I tore up and typed out again? Whatever should I feel like if one got printed?'

Aunt Grace laughed. 'You wait and see,' she said. 'It will be a lovely feeling, I can tell you.'

So Lizzie put her three stories into a big envelope. She typed another envelope to herself, in case the stories were sent back: *Miss Elizabeth Farrell, House at the Corner, Rivers-End*. Miss Elizabeth Farrell. Such a different person from plain Lizzie! Suppose she saw her full name printed at the end of one of the stories? She would die of pride and happiness!

She went out to post the stories. Greta met her in the hall. 'I will post for you, Lizzie,' she said, in her usual kindly way. She always loved to do any little thing for the family.

'No, I'll go, Greta,' said Lizzie, smiling. 'It's something rather important and I want to wish it luck when the letter goes plop into the pillar-box!'

'I wish it luck also then!' said Greta, her eyes beaming. 'Great good luck! You will tell me if the great good luck comes, Lizzie?'

'Perhaps I will,' said Lizzie, and went off to the post, thinking that Greta would certainly rejoice as much as anyone if her stories were really successful.

10

A Wonderful Surprise

One afternoon, when Lizzie was at school, Aunt Grace went to put Sukie the parrot into the shade, for the sun was very hot. June was in now, and was living up to its old name of 'flaming June'.

The postman came up as Aunt Grace dragged the heavy cage into the shade. He gave her a hand.

'Where's your hanky?' Sukie said to him and made him laugh.

'Thank you,' said Aunt Grace. 'Oh, what a lot of letters!'

She took the pile from the postman and he went down the path to the front gate, hearing Sukie calling out after him. 'Where's your hanky? Hip-hip, hooray!'

Aunt Grace looked through the letters to see if there were any for her. Yes, two, good. Five for John – three for Lucy – one for the twins from that nice friend of theirs, Michael. One for Tony, none for Pam – and one for Lizzie.

It was addressed to Miss Elizabeth Farrell, and was typed. It was an ordinary envelope, but on the back flap were stamped the letters R-E.W.

In a flash Aunt Grace knew what the letters stood for – *Rivers-End Weekly*. It was a letter from the local paper – a letter – without returned stories in, for the envelope was too small to contain them.

It could only mean that the editor of the paper was interested in Lizzie's stories. What did he say in the letter? Aunt Grace could hardly wait for Lizzie to come home from school that day!

At last she saw Lizzie coming home on her bicycle. She ran after her to the shed with the precious letter. 'Hello, Aunt Grace!' said Lizzie. 'You look excited. Anything happened?'

'There's a letter for you, it's from the *Rivers-End Weekly*,' said Aunt Grace. 'Here it is.'

Lizzie opened the letter with fingers that suddenly trembled. Suppose – oh suppose – no, don't suppose! It was probably only to say that the stories were no good.

She shook out the small, folded piece of typed paper inside. She and Aunt Grace read it together:

Dear Miss Farrell,

We thank you for sending us your three stories, which we like very much. We own six other weekly papers, appearing in different districts, and we would like to be able to print your stories weekly, in each of these papers. We should like to arrange with you to send us in one each week. Payment will be at our usual rates, and a cheque will be sent on publication. We propose to print the first story next week.

Yours faithfully,
H. Bruce, Editor.

Lizzie's eyes grew misty behind their glasses and she swallowed hard. Her mouth trembled and she could hardly speak. 'Aunt Grace,' she whispered, 'oh Aunt Grace!'

Aunt Grace was just as much overcome as Lizzie. She dabbed at her eyes hurriedly with her handkerchief, and cleared her throat. Then she gave Lizzie a sudden hug.

'Oh, how lovely!' she said. 'Congratulations, my dear, you deserve it. But fancy – a story every single week. Can you do it?'

'I can try,' said Lizzie. 'But Aunt Grace, are they going to *pay* me? I never thought of that! I just thought of the joy of seeing my stories in print with my name on them. I never thought of being *paid*.'

'Oh, of course, you'll be paid,' said Aunt Grace, laughing at Lizzie's amazed face. 'How do you think writers live if they aren't paid for their work like other people? How long were those stories, Lizzie?'

'About fifteen hundred words each,' said Lizzie. 'What will they pay me?'

'Two or three pounds, I should think,' said Aunt Grace, 'especially as they are printing them in other papers at the same time. You've made a beginning, Lizzie – and so soon too.'

'But I nearly didn't,' said Lizzie. 'When I tore that first story up and threw the bits in Tony's face, I made up my mind never to try again, never. And if it hadn't been for you, I wouldn't have, either, Aunt Grace. Oh – isn't it wonderful!'

'Come and tell the others,' said Aunt Grace and pulled her hand. But Lizzie shook her head.

'No,' she said. 'No – not yet, anyway. Let me enjoy it all to myself for a bit. They might laugh. And anyway I'd rather wait till the first story comes out, Aunt Grace – with my name on. Elizabeth Farrell – I shall *really* feel like Elizabeth then, somebody who's done something and is going on to do much, much more!'

'Well, it's your secret, child,' said Aunt Grace. 'But let your family share your joy as soon as you can.'

'That's just it, I don't believe most of them will share it!' said Lizzie. 'Pam will be jealous, Tony will laugh and say something smart that will make the others laugh too, and Mummy won't understand why I want to call myself Elizabeth Farrell. They might just spoil things, Aunt Grace. I must wait a bit and enjoy it all in secret myself first.'

'I'll enjoy it with you,' said Aunt Grace, and gave Lizzie another hug. 'You're a nice child, Lizzie, you deserve a bit of luck.'

Lizzie could hardly believe her news. She kept the letter in her pocket and opened it to read again and again when she was by herself. Her eyes shone happily and her mouth smiled all the evening. She had had a story – three stories – taken by a paper. They wanted one every week. She, Elizabeth Farrell, was a writer, somebody who could earn money and who would see her own name in print. She didn't stop thinking of it once, and Aunt Grace, watching her, was glad of the girl's sudden happiness.

She looks quite pretty tonight, she thought. Without her glasses and that wire round her teeth, she would look a darling. Pam's as pretty as a picture, but her scowl does spoil her so, and her mouth is getting such a downward curve. Lizzie for me every time!

Greta noticed Lizzie's smiling eyes that night. She stopped and spoke to the girl when she saw her alone for a moment. 'You have had your great good luck?' she said, in her pretty Austrian voice. 'Your eyes tell me so, Lizzie!'

'Yes, Greta, I got the good luck!' said Lizzie, in an exultant tone. 'Can't tell you about it yet – but I will.'

'I am glad for you, vairy, vairy glad,' said warm-hearted Greta. 'I will give you a piece of my chocolate to show you I am glad for you!'

'No, Greta! You've given most of it to the twins already!' said Lizzie, catching hold of Greta's arm. 'Beside, I couldn't eat anything tonight. I'm too excited.'

All the same she found a piece of Greta's delicious Austrian chocolate on her dressing-table that night when she went to bed. Poor Greta – how she did try to 'belong' to this English family, to feel that she had a place there, to

share their sadness and gladness just as she had once shared in her own vanished family's sorrows and joys.

Nobody took much notice of Lizzie those days, though her shining eyes gave away the fact that something big had happened to her. Everyone was getting worked up about Pam's play! Tony heard her part for her time and again. Lizzie and Jean sewed hard at the beautiful trailing clothes she was to wear. Mrs Farrell listened endlessly to accounts of all the rehearsals, the stupidity of Angela who always had to be prompted, the way Katie always forgot to come on to the stage at exactly the right moment, the beautiful new stage curtains that someone had presented to the school, the row there was when somebody began to giggle at the rehearsal . . . in fact, nobody was allowed to think or talk of anything but the wonderful play!

'When is the scholarship exam?' asked Aunt Grace, interrupting Pam's excited account of how Miss Romula had praised her acting that day.

'It's this week,' said Pam, frowning at the interruption. 'Well, as I said . . .'

'This week!' said Aunt Grace, in surprise. 'Well, you never said a word about it, Pam! How are you getting on with the exam papers?'

'Fine, of course,' said Pam, impatiently. 'I don't mind exams, Aunt Grace. I'm not one of those people who gets all nervous and upset in exams like Lizzie. She never can do a thing in exams, never gets top marks even if she knows the subject inside out. Goes all flop.'

'Can't think why,' said Tony. 'I love exams. Give you a chance of showing off your brains!'

'Well, you don't seem to have shown off yours much, judging by the results last term,' said Aunt Grace, remembering the report she had seen.

'Oh, Aunt Grace, don't nag at a fellow!' groaned Tony. 'You're always getting a dig in somewhere. Nobody bothers to work in old Blinky's form, I tell you. I'll work all right with Snorter. Have to!'

'Well, I only hope Pam isn't giving too much attention to this play and not enough to her exam,' said Aunt Grace, going on with her knitting. 'It would be simply dreadful if she failed to win the scholarship, after all our hopes.'

'Oh Aunt Grace, it wouldn't matter a bit if I didn't get it,' said Pam, exasperated. 'Not a bit. I'm going to college anyhow. Father's got the money to pay for me whether I win the scholarship or not. I'm safe. I'd just like to win it to show everyone how easy it is. I've always passed with honours any exam I've taken.'

The twins came in from the garden, hot and dirty. Pam looked at them in disgust. 'What have you been doing? You smell awful.'

'Cleaning out the hen-house,' said David. 'It's rather a smelly job but we like it. Mum, the hen-house looks marvellous now. You really ought to go and see it. Can I whitewash it inside, please? Frost says he hasn't got time.'

'Mother, make them go and have a bath, and change,' groaned Pam. 'They smell horrible. Why must they go and wallow in hen-houses and things?'

105

'The hen-house is lovely now,' said Delia. 'Do come and see it, Pam.'

'I never go near the hens if I can help it,' said Pam, turning up her nose. 'Smelly things with fleas all over them!'

'They haven't got fleas!' said Delia, indignantly. 'They're the cleanest hens in Rivers-End. Mummy, do come and see how nicely we've done the hen-house.'

'I will sometime, dear,' said Mrs Farrell.

'You always say that,' said David, 'and you hardly ever *do* come and see what we've done.'

'Don't be cheeky,' said Pam, sharply.

'I'm not,' said David, in surprise. 'It's quite true what I say – nobody ever comes to see what we've been doing or takes an interest in it. But everybody goes cracked over your old play!'

Aunt Grace laughed out loud, suddenly. Solemn, out-spoken, hard-working David always amused her. But he was too serious and solemn. It would do him and Delia good to go to boarding-school and mix with hordes of children all with the same interests, all with the same love of nature and animals and gardening. They kept themselves to themselves too much.

'Aunt Grace, you shouldn't encourage the twins to be rude,' began Pam, enraged. 'Really, I think it's too—'

'Hold your tongue, Pamela,' said Aunt Grace,

sharply. 'I'm an old woman and I won't be put in my place by a snippet like you. If I didn't think you were really working much too hard, I'd say a lot more.'

Pam went crimson. The twins giggled and went out to have a bath, leaving an aroma of hens behind them. Lizzie looked upset for a minute and then, remembering her good fortune, smiled to herself again. Tony went out whistling. Mrs Farrell sighed and thought that a family was very, very difficult.

Aunt Grace knitted hard. She knitted all her annoyance into the sock and felt very much better afterwards.

11

The Story is Printed

The scholarship exam was over. Pam had hardly realised it had come and gone, for even in the midst of answering exam questions she had been dreaming of the play.

She would look so beautiful! How all the small girls would sigh and clap and cheer! How the parents would applaud her! And even Miss Dawes the head would think what a wonderful girl, she, Pam, was.

'She took the scholarship exam in her stride,' Miss Dawes would say. 'Won it and hardly thought about it, she was so busy with the school play. One of the most brilliant girls I have ever had. I prophesy a wonderful career for her.'

June was over now, and there were only three more weeks till the end of the term. Not much more time to rehearse for the play but Pam didn't mind. She was quite ready. Her dresses were finished. If only stupid Angela would learn her part properly!

Tony was still waiting to play his wonderful trick on old Blinky. He had heard that the head was going away for a few days before the end of term – that would be the best time to play the trick. Then he would be certain that the head would not come wandering in unexpectedly, sniffing the terrible smell himself. All the boys in the form were eager for Tony to play his trick. What a laugh they would have!

Lizzie was still in the seventh heaven of delight, eagerly waiting for Thursday, when the issue of the paper would be published which would print her first story. What *would* the others say when they saw her name at the end?

It seemed as if Thursday would never come, but it dawned at last. Lizzie hardly slept all that night. She was down long before breakfast, waiting for the papers. Greta was astonished.

'Ah, you wait for another letter?' she said, beaming. But Lizzie shook her head.

'No, I just want to have a look at one of the papers before the others get it,' she said. 'Ah, there's the paperboy now.'

The papers came through the big letterbox, one after the other. Daddy's paper – Mother's paper – Aunt Grace's paper – the weekly magazine for the twins – and – the *Rivers-End Weekly*.

She picked it up and ran to her room, looking feverishly through the big sheets. Ah, 'Children's Corner'. Here it was. 'The Story of the Thirteen Cats.' Yes, they had printed it, really printed it!

Lizzie sat down on her bed and read the story through, very slowly. It sounded good – it *was* good! Surely everyone would think it was good and would read it to their children?

Then her heart almost stopped. She had read very slowly, saving up for herself the delicious shock of seeing her name at the end – Elizabeth Farrell – and it wasn't there!

It wasn't there. There was no name at the end at all. They hadn't bothered to print the name of the author. The story might have been written by anybody. Nobody would guess who had really written it. Perhaps they hadn't thought much of it after all – hadn't thought it was worth printing the author's name at the end.

Lizzie was terribly disappointed. Most of her joy had been in looking forward to seeing her own name in print, not only her story. She had wanted to show the story to the others with her name clearly there. Now she couldn't. Would they believe it was by her? Wouldn't Tony laugh one of his scornful little laughs, and say she was pulling his leg? Yes, he would.

She knocked at Aunt Grace's door and went in. The old lady was still in bed, drinking her morning tea. She was surprised to see Lizzie's disappointed face.

'They've got my story in – but they've left out my name,' said poor Lizzie, her voice shaking a little. 'Nobody will believe it's mine now.'

'Well, who would have thought of that?' said Aunt Grace, surprised. She read the story. 'It reads very well, doesn't it, Lizzie. Cheer up. You've really and truly got a story in print and that's a marvellous thing, maybe they will print your name next time. It was probably overlooked. Now, when are you going to tell everyone? At breakfast-time?'

'Oh no,' said Lizzie, scared at the thought of making such an announcement at table. 'No. I'll tell you what I'll do, Aunt Grace. I'll get the others to read the story and then, when they've all read it, I'll say I wrote it. Make it a kind of surprise for them.'

So after breakfast Lizzie took the paper to her mother. 'Mummy, do read this little story, will you? And ask Daddy to read it too. Please do.'

'Very well, dear. Later on,' said Mrs Farrell, vaguely. 'Put it down there. Why, is it a very good story? I never think the stories are worth reading in this paper.'

'What's this wonderful story?' said Pam, and she ran her eyes down it. 'Golly, what a soppy story! I should think the person who wrote it must be batty!'

Lizzie went red. She stared in distress at Pam. Pam didn't know that she, Lizzie, had written it. She had called the story soppy – that was how

111

it struck her – and perhaps that was how it would strike most people. She wished she hadn't asked her mother to read it.

'Come on, Lizzie, we must get off to school or we shall be awfully late,' said Pam, looking at the clock. 'We've a rehearsal this morning. Hope that idiot Angela has learned her words properly for once!'

They went off. Lizzie thought of her printed story all the morning. She wondered what her mother would say about it. Surely her mother would like it? She didn't care what Pam said, it was a good story. Pam always sneered at everything. So did Tony.

'Mummy, did you read that story?' she asked anxiously, when she got back at one o'clock. Mrs Farrell looked up. She had looked through the paper that morning and had remembered that Lizzie had asked her to read a story. But Mrs Farrell had read the wrong story! She had not read the children's story, but a story written for grown-ups, and she hadn't liked it at all.

'Yes, dear, I read the story,' she said. 'It was a silly story, I thought. I'm surprised you wanted me to read it. I didn't ask Daddy to read it, because he hasn't time for such nonsense. I don't consider it was worth reading.'

Lizzie's heart sank into her boots. She was glad there was no one else in the room. She was glad that she had not told anyone but Aunt Grace that her story was in the paper. How dreadful to write a story that everyone thought was silly! She was glad now that her name was not at the end.

She was very sad that day. Aunt Grace had gone out for the day to see a friend, or she would have comforted Lizzie. All the pleasure of seeing her story in print was spoilt. She did not for a moment guess that her mother had not read the right story. Poor Lizzie!

By the afternoon post there was an envelope marked R-E.W. again. Lizzie opened it and inside was a cheque for three pounds. The girl stared at it disbelievingly. Three whole pounds! For one story! It simply couldn't be true.

But it was. Lizzie took it up to her bedroom and stared at it. Why, she was rich! If she got three pounds every single week, what a lot of things she could do! She could buy the most wonderful birthday and Christmas presents for everyone! She could buy Aunt Grace something really lovely for helping her so much. She could buy her mother that electric clock she was always saying she would like to get.

'But I shan't tell anyone where I'm getting the money from!' said Lizzie. 'Only Aunt Grace, and she's got to know. They can all think the stories are silly, and think the writer of them is batty if they like – I shan't tell them anything about my stories at all – but I'll spend my money on them and give them lovely surprises. I shan't let anybody guess my secret at all.'

Aunt Grace was delighted to see the cheque. 'What does your mother say?' she asked.

'I haven't told anyone, Aunt Grace,' said Lizzie. 'And I don't want to. I've decided not to tell anyone that those weekly children's stories are mine, either. Pam thought the one in today was – was – soppy – and Mummy thought it was silly – so . . .'

'Oh, Lizzie! But they wouldn't have thought or said that if they'd known the story was yours!' cried Aunt Grace.

'I don't want them to think a story is good

just because I wrote it,' said Lizzie, in her most obstinate voice. 'I want them to think it's good anyhow, and to be proud of it. You don't understand, Aunt Grace.'

But Aunt Grace did understand. It was too bad of that spiteful little Pam to make fun of the story. And what a pity Mrs Farrell had called it silly. Aunt Grace couldn't understand that. The story was anything but silly. She sighed. This Farrell family didn't pull together at all. They didn't back one another up.

'I'll change your cheque for you, dear,' she said to Lizzie. 'You sign it – here on the back, look – and I'll pay it into my bank, and give you three pounds in cash for it. Fancy, Lizzie, every week, it's simply marvellous!'

But Lizzie would not smile. She meant to spend the money on her family but she felt resentful towards them. If only they had liked her story and had exclaimed over it and patted her on the back. If only they could have seen that she wasn't just plain little Lizzie but clever Elizabeth Farrell just for once.

But they hadn't and they never would. So she would just go on being Elizabeth to herself, and one day perhaps she would be such a famous writer that even her own family would call her Elizabeth and treat her differently!

But she had a nice little surprise that night

when Delia and David got hold of the weekly paper and looked for the Children's Corner.

'I say, there's a jolly good story this week!' said Delia. 'Much better than the tripe they usually put in. It's one that Lizzie sometimes used to tell us. Read it, Dave!'

David read it and pronounced it good stuff. Lizzie glowed and suddenly felt very much better. Delia and David ought to know if it was good – it was written for children!

'I'll cut it out and keep it,' said Delia's clear voice. 'I like it. Pam, read it.'

'I've read it, thanks,' said Pam. 'Soppy stuff, I think! Give it to Lizzie. It's more her style than mine!'

It was nice to watch the twins cutting out her story. She longed to tell them who had written

it. But that little hard core of anger that was still in her heart would not let her say anything. She sat at her work and said nothing.

'You know that trick I told you I was going to play on old Blinky, don't you?' said Tony, suddenly, to the other four children, when they were all alone in their playroom. 'Well, it's coming off tomorrow!'

'Good luck to you,' said Pam. The twins giggled. They had smelled the dreadful smell, and wondered what in the world old Blinky would say when he smelled it.

'The head's going away tomorrow for a day or two,' said Tony. 'So it's a good chance to play the trick. Make old Blinky sit up, won't it?'

'You don't seem to do anything but play about in Blinky's class,' said Lizzie. 'Nobody would dare to do things like that in my class. We'd be sent out to the head at once.'

'Pooh – you're a goody-goody lot, anyway,' said Tony. 'And not one of you has the brains to think out a thumping good joke. Golly, I'm longing for tomorrow! Old Blinky simply won't believe in a smell like that!'

'Well, I'll be glad when you take the smell out of the house,' said Pam. 'It's a hundred times worse than the hen-house!'

'I'll tell you what happens tomorrow,' said Tony. 'We'll have some fun, I can tell you!'

12

Tony plays his Trick

The next day the boys in Tony's form were full of delighted anticipation. Tony was really going to play his trick at last. The head was not at Prayers that morning. It would be quite safe to play it.

Not a scrap of work was done in Mr Holmes's class in the first two lessons. The master, a scholarly, mild man, quite unable to deal with boys like Tony, sensed the excitement and sighed. He had been able to get on fairly well until Tony had come into his class. How he disliked that boy! Always pulling his leg, slacking, making the others laugh and slack too.

The trick was to be played in the lesson before Break. It was an English lesson. The class was doing Shakespeare's *Henry V*, and had been taking the different parts. Today Mr Holmes planned to explain many of the old words and write their meanings on the board.

The boys settled into their places, eager and excited. Tony was in one of the front desks, the 'smell-bottle' held between his legs, his small sprayer in his desk, ready to get out when the chance came. Every master made Tony sit in the front so that he could be safely under the teacher's eyes.

'Well, boys, we will not read out parts today, but will give a little time to discovering the meaning of some of the old words,' began Blinky, looking short-sightedly through his glasses. The lenses magnified his eyes very much, and made him look rather owlish. 'Turn to page – er – page sixty-four, please. There you will find . . .' Boys coughed and fidgeted. Someone opened his desk and let the lid bang loudly, making Blinky jump. He had never got used to desk-banging. He looked across at the boy who had dropped his desk lid so violently.

'Rawlings! Don't do that.'

'Sorry, sir. Lid slipped, sir. Like this, sir,' said Rawlings and, opening his desk, he let the lid bang again. 'No, not quite like that, sir – like this . . .'

Boys laughed loudly. Tony grinned. Rawlings was his best friend and could always be relied on to provide a few laughs.

'Enough, Rawlings,' said Blinky. 'Now – as I was saying – these old words . . .'

He went on for a few minutes. Tony put up his hand. 'Please, sir, it would be a help if you listed them on the board. We could copy them down, and . . .'

'Just what I was going to do,' said Blinky and turned to the board. He took up the chalk and began to write in his slow, upright writing.

'Quick! Now!' whispered Rawlings. 'Go on, Farrell!'

Tony grinned again. He took his sprayer quietly out of his desk, slipped the cork out of the bottle and filled the sprayer. He put the cork back into the bottle at once, for he did not want to be choked by the awful smell. As it was, he had to hold his breath for a minute.

Blinky was still slowly writing his words. Tony reached out over his desk and suddenly and quietly sprayed some of his terrible concoction in a fine mist towards Blinky. The window happened to be wide open and a breeze blew in, taking the mist towards the blackboard.

Blinky suddenly got a whiff. He stood still, startled, the chalk held upright in his hand. He sniffed cautiously and almost choked. What in the world was that frightful smell? He had never smelled anything like it in his life!

He made a choking noise. The boys heard him and grinned in delight. It was beginning! Blinky turned round and got another whiff. To his intense surprise none of the boys seemed to smell what he was smelling. This was not surprising as Tony had been careful to spray the smell right away from the class.

Blinky stared at the boys, swallowing hard, trying not to sniff any more of the frightful smell. 'Er – er can you boys smell something – er – something really horrible?' began poor Blinky, and choked into his handkerchief.

Tony answered for the form. He could keep a perfectly straight face when he wanted to. His face was quite solemn and serious now as he answered Blinky.

'What do you mean, sir? A horrible smell? No – there doesn't seem to be one.' He sniffed loudly. That was the signal for everyone to do the same, and immediately the classroom was filled with the sound of thirty boys sniffing vigorously, their noses in the air.

'Nothing to smell, sir,' reported Tony, after a spate of terrific sniffing. One or two boys

121

sniggered and Tony looked round, frowning. He didn't want Blinky to guess it was a trick.

Blinky took his handkerchief away from his nose and sniffed delicately and cautiously, like a cat, afraid to sniff too strongly in case he was overwhelmed by that incredible smell again. To his immense relief he could no longer smell the horrible odour.

'It seems to have gone,' said Blinky, taking a long breath. He went to the window and leaned out, feeling quite overcome by his experience. What a truly terrible smell! What could it have been? Were the drains of the school blocked up, or something? Could there be a dead rat somewhere?

One or two boys, unable to contain themselves, took the chance of exploding into their handkerchiefs whilst Blinky was leaning out of the window. But when the master returned to his place, the class appeared to be politely awaiting him. He took up the chalk again.

'Now let me see – ah, yes – I was just writing the meaning of the word . . .' he began again, and the chalk once more scraped on the board.

Quick as a flash Tony sprayed some more of the liquid and the fine mist evaporated in the air round poor Blinky, leaving behind it the same astounding smell. It descended on Blinky and left him petrified. He stood there hardly daring to breathe. That smell again! He would be sick – he would faint. There couldn't be such a smell in the world!

Blinky choked and gasped, spluttered and put his hands over his face. He reeled to the window and hung his head out in the fresh breeze. The boys exploded. Rawlings held his side, his face purple. Tony yelled too. Everyone did. The trick was an even greater success than they had dared to hope.

Blinky, intent on getting away from the fearful stench, at first heard nothing of the uproar. Then he pulled himself together, stood up and faced the boys. Behind his glasses his eyes glinted angrily.

'Boys! Boys! Stop this noise at once! I dare say it is funny to you, but I can only be glad that you have not experienced this truly terrible smell. Extraordinary! Most astounding. I must get the head to have the school drains examined at once. There must be a leakage somewhere.'

Sniffing delicately again Blinky returned to his desk. He was relieved to find that the smell had apparently gone again. He sniffed round the wall, wondering if the smell came from behind it. The boys sniggered again. This was the very best joke Tony Farrell had ever played. Rawlings leaned over and nudged him. 'Do it again!' he whispered. 'Go on – while he's sniffing about.'

Tony could not resist having another shot with the sprayer. He filled it cautiously and sent out another fine mist over Blinky's turned back. To the master's horror he was enveloped for the third time in the unbelievable smell. It was worse than bad drains, worse than dead rats, worse than anything he had ever imagined in his most vivid nightmare.

He clutched at his desk and choked. He sat down in his chair and almost fainted. Then he staggered to the window again. A faint echo of the smell came with him and the boys he passed shrank back. 'Phew!' said Rawlings, turning pale. 'What a stink!'

Blinky hung out of the window, panting and spluttering at the same time. The boys began to laugh again, and Rawlings, recovering from the whiff he had had, let out his great guffaw of laughter. 'Haw-haw-haw, haw-haw! Haw-haw-haw-haw!'

He had a tremendous laugh, well-known all over the school. It was most infectious and the boys roared all the more when they heard it. Little Brown, overcome with his mirth, rolled off his chair on to the floor and kicked his legs in the air.

Mr Holmes could do nothing to stop them. He was still trying to recover from the poisonous stench he had breathed into his lungs. But in the class next door was Mr Lehman, second only to the head himself. He was taking scripture, and was already amazed by the continual sounds of mirth that had been coming from Blinky's classroom for some time.

Mr Lehman's class listened in surprise too. It was nothing new to hear noises in Mr Holmes's form – everyone knew that he wasn't much good at keeping order – but no one had ever heard such terrific bursts of laughter before.

'Hark at old Rawlings!' whispered one boy to another. 'Just hark at him! Whatever's happening?'

Mr Lehman could not imagine what was going on next door but he judged that it was certainly time for him to find out. Mr Holmes's classes were known to be disorderly, but really, it was too much this morning! Why, he could hardly hear himself speak. Pity the head was away, or he might have heard the row himself and gone to inquire about it! Mr Lehman felt pretty certain that that boy Farrell was at the bottom of the disturbance. Wretched boy – no sense of responsibility or decency at all.

Mr Lehman strode to the door and opened it. He marched down the corridor. He came to the door of Blinky's room from behind which screeches, cackles and guffaws were still coming. He flung it open, white with rage.

At first the boys did not notice him. Neither did Mr Holmes, for he was still leaning out of the window. Mr Lehman gazed in astonishment at the sight of the sprawling, yelling boys. Were they mad? And where was Mr Holmes?

With a shock the boys suddenly saw Mr Lehman. Williams nudged Brown. 'Get up, idiot, Lehman's here!' Harris poked Rawlings. 'Shut up, fool, here's Lehman.' Fielding shook Tony. 'Look, Farrell, there's Lehman.'

One by one the boys sobered up, sat properly in their seats, and gazed in fright at Mr Lehman's set and angry face. They were scared of him. He was as good a disciplinarian as Blinky was a bad one. He was more feared than either Snorter or the head – what bad luck that he should have heard the row!

Tony wished he had not got the smell-bottle with him. Suppose Mr Lehman saw it! He would be caught red-handed then. He glanced at the window. He would throw the bottle out as soon as he got the chance – when Mr Lehman turned away for a moment.

Mr Holmes staggered away from the window, feeling better for the fresh air. He saw Mr Lehman and gulped.

'I came to see what the extraordinary noise was,' said Mr Lehman, coldly. 'I couldn't hear myself speak.'

'It was the smell,' said poor Mr Holmes. 'The most terrible stench I have ever smelled in my life, Lehman. Over here, by the blackboard. Made me choke and . . .'

Mr Lehman strode over to the blackboard. There was no smell at all left by then. He sniffed hard and looked at Mr Holmes. 'I can smell nothing,' he said. 'Nothing!'

An uncontrollable giggle came from poor Brown, who, once he had really let himself go, found it almost impossible to stop. A thought struck Mr Lehman. Was it one of those obnoxious tricks being played by that clever scamp, Tony Farrell? He glared at Tony, who looked back, feeling most uncomfortable and wishing that the smell-bottle was anywhere but between his knees.

Mr Lehman turned to Blinky and quick as a flash Tony raised his arm and flung the smell-bottle deftly out of the open window. Thank goodness, it was gone. Now not even old Lehman could trace the trick to him!

13

A Shock for Tony

The bottle flew out of the window. Tony's classroom was on the second floor of the big school building, and the window overlooked the playground. The boys listened for the smash.

There was a thud and a high scream! Then silence. Mr Lehman, startled at the anguished cry, strode to the window. He looked out. Down below, on the playground, lay a small boy, quite still. Over him bent another small boy, evidently very frightened. Mr Lehman called down.

'Hey there – what's the matter?'

The small boy looked up. It was David. He saw Mr Lehman and called up to him.

'Oh sir, I don't know! I was crossing the playground with Walters, taking a message, when Walters suddenly screamed and fell down. Something's hit him on the head, sir; he's bleeding – and oh sir – there's a most terrible smell!'

'Stay there, young Farrell, and I'll come down,' called Mr Lehman. David stayed where he was, unable any longer to bend over his friend Walters because of the unendurable smell that suddenly enveloped them. He had not seen the broken smell-bottle, and did not even know that it had hit Walters on the head. He was white and frightened.

Mr Lehman went down, called to Mrs Kenton, the head's wife, as he passed her door, 'There's a boy hurt, Mrs Kenton, can you come?'

Mrs Kenton rushed after him. Soon they were bending over the unconscious boy – but immediately they drew back because of the frightful smell round him.

Mr Lehman dragged the boy out of it and then lifted him up a little. There was a terrible cut on his head. Just near him lay the fragments of the bottle. At first the master and Mrs Kenton

were too much concerned with the injured boy to take any notice of the broken glass.

'We must get the doctor,' said Mrs Kenton. She glanced at David. 'David – you can telephone, can't you? Go and ring up the school doctor at once. Hurry!'

David sped off, glad of something to do. What could have happened? Why, he and Walters were just walking quietly along when something struck poor old Walters on the head and he gave that awful scream and fell down like a stone.

Upstairs, on the second floor, in Blinky's classroom, a dead silence reigned. Nobody had been able to hear quite what David had shouted. Nobody knew what had happened, and they were longing to know. Rawlings thought with relief that it was a good thing something had happened to turn old Lehman's attention away from their class. Perhaps he would forget about the row.

In the ordinary way half the boys would have shot to the window and leaned out. But they were scared now, and nobody moved. Mr Holmes went to the window himself, but could not make out what had happened. Some sort of accident, evidently. Well, Lehman was there, and Mrs Kenton too. He had better get on with the lesson.

He faced a very subdued class indeed. Even

young Brown had sobered up completely. Tony looked scared. He hoped that nobody would find his smashed smell-bottle, wherever it had landed. He did not know that it had hit anyone. The playground was usually deserted at that time of the morning. What bad luck that Lehman had come in like that!

Mr Holmes was feeling weak and upset. He felt that he could not say more than a few words. Thank goodness it was practically time for Break.

'Please read the whole of the next scene,' he said, weakly, and the boys, quiet and obedient, set to work, hardly able to see what they were reading, each fearing in his mind the wrath of Mr Lehman.

It was a great relief when the bell clanged loudly for Break. Tony's form raced out, eager to find out what had been happening in the playground below. David came up to Tony and pulled at his arm. His eyes were full of tears, which he tried in vain to keep back.

'I want to speak to you, Tony. Tony, listen,' said David, in an urgent voice. 'Something dreadful's happened!'

'What?' asked Tony, impatiently.

'Well, I was walking across the playground with Walters – you know, Tom Walters, my friend – and suddenly something flew down and hit him on the head and he fell down, bleeding.

And then there was a most frightful smell.'

Tony stared at David, his heart sinking. He saw at once what had happened. His smell-bottle – it had struck poor little Tom Walters!

'And Tony, I had to ring up the doctor – and he came – and he's taken Tom to – to – the hospital,' said David, in a trembling voice, a tear running to the tip of his turned-up nose. 'Oh Tony, will he die?'

Tony went very pale. He took David to a quiet corner and the boys sat down on a bench there. Tony did not know what to say. This was a real disaster, a most terrible thing, but he hadn't meant to do it.

David thought that Tony's silence meant that he was certain poor Tom would die and he burst into tears. 'Oh Tony, he looked so awful lying there quite still – and he was b-b-bleeding – and that awful smell . . .'

'Shut up,' said Tony, in a choking voice. 'David, don't say anything to anyone about the smell.'

David stared at Tony in sudden horror. His eyes grew wide. 'Tony! Tony – it wasn't your smell-bottle, was it? Tony?'

'I tell you, shut up about it,' said Tony, cruel in his terrible anxiety over what he had done. 'Shut up, you silly idiot, shut up!'

He got up and left David. The small boy

stared after him, horrified and grieved. His mind was in a turmoil and he longed for Delia.

Tony went off by himself, his mind in much more of a turmoil than David's. He was filled with horror, his bottle had hit young Walters, but he hadn't meant it so surely nobody could blame him very much? But suppose Walters died; suppose he was badly injured even? What would the head say? And Mr Walters, who was a stern, outspoken man. And his own father and mother! It was a black and terrible time for Tony the light-hearted, Tony the joker, the mirth-maker.

The other boys had heard the news now, and although nothing had been said to them by David about the bottle, they guessed. They looked at Tony as they went back into class. They nudged one another. Tony had injured

young Walters. What was he going to do about it? Was he going to own up – make a clean breast of the whole joke – what was he going to do?

Just as they had followed and admired and applauded Tony when he was acting the fool, so now they avoided him and even looked at him with scorn because things had gone wrong. Tony was amazed and hurt. Why should they all desert him now, just because something had happened that he couldn't help? Only Rawlings seemed still to be really friendly.

Tony did not know that he had no real friends. None of the masters respected him or even liked him. The boys laughed in delight at his fooling and clever tricks but they did not really admire his character or trust him. He was to find that out now, and it was very bitter to him indeed. He wanted friends now, he wanted someone to say, 'Cheer up, it won't be so bad. Walters will soon be all right. I'll stick up for you!'

But not even Rawlings did that. Rawlings just talked to him as usual and did not mention young Walters, or try to ease the awful anxiety that was gnawing at his heart.

The whole class was so easy to manage for the rest of the morning that Blinky was amazed. He had not seen Mr Lehman again, and he hoped that the master would say no more about the disturbance and not report it to the head.

At the end of the morning Tony rode home on his bicycle, and on the way he caught up with David. 'Any news of Walters?' he asked gruffly.

'No. I'm going to ask Mum to ring up and ask about him,' said David, pedalling furiously. 'Oh, Tony, it's all dreadful. Tony, I won't say anything about that bottle if you don't want me to – except to Delia – but Tony, you're going to own up about it, aren't you?'

'It's none of your business, David,' said Tony, even more gruffly. 'See? It wasn't really my fault, you know that. Anyway, the head's away, so the whole thing may blow over.'

'But Tony, Tom's badly hurt!' said David. 'You forget that. You did it to him, even though you didn't mean to. You ought to go to Mrs Walters – you ought to ask about Tom yourself – you ought to—'

'You shut up,' said Tony, unable to bear any more instructions from David, partly because he knew his small brother was quite right. But he was afraid. Terribly afraid. Afraid of what this person might say and that person. He must just lie low for a day or two and perhaps the whole thing would pass over, the masters wouldn't guess it was he, Tony, at the bottom of everything.

'You're playing the coward!' said David, and

rode away quickly to avoid the kick that the exasperated Tony tried to give him.

David told Delia the whole story. She listened in horror. But both she and David were completely loyal to Tony and said nothing whatever about his part in the accident. David told his mother that Tom Walters was in hospital and asked her to ring up and find out if he was all right.

But there was no news to be had, except that an operation had had to be done on his head. 'In fact,' said the nurse, 'it is being done now – by your husband, I believe, Mrs Farrell. No doubt he will tell you all about it when he comes home.'

Tony could hardly wait for his father to come back. David went to meet him. 'Daddy! Is Tom all right? Is he very bad?'

'Bad enough, poor lad,' said Mr Farrell, coming into the dining-room. 'But he'll be all right. I've dealt with that damaged head of his, but it will be some time before he can get out of the hospital. What a thing to happen! I can't make out exactly what did happen – nobody seems to know. You were with him, weren't you, David?'

'Yes. I was there,' said David, and glanced at Tony, who was sitting very still and white at the table. Tony looked at David beseechingly, hoping and praying that the boy was not going to tell the whole story. David waited for Tony to take the chance of explaining, but the boy was silent.

'It seems as if somebody must have thrown a bottle out of one of the second or third floor windows,' said Mr Farrell, tucking into peas and new potatoes. 'Wicked thing to do! Whoever did it ought to be severely punished. Might have killed young Tom. I should be very sorry if any son of mine did such a stupid and dangerous thing.'

'Oh, John, of course none of our children would ever do a thing like that!' said Mrs Farrell, indignantly. David choked over his lunch, and Tony tried in vain to swallow his mouthful. How could he ever eat his plateful of meat, potatoes and peas? What a terrible feeling this was that he had inside him; shame and fear and worry and dread! Would it ever go away?

'I suppose an inquiry will be made into the whole affair,' said Mr Farrell. 'I hope there will be. Dangerous foolery like that should be stopped. Pity the head's away, or he would have gone into things at once. These peas are most delicious, Lucy. I must say Greta's a very fine cook.'

Tony was thankful to have the subject changed. Lizzie noticed how silent he was and looked at him in alarm. Was he ill? He didn't seem to be eating his lunch very fast.

'Are you all right, Tony?' she asked in a low voice. She got a scowl from her brother in reply. Mrs Farrell looked up.

'Tony, you do look rather white,' she said. 'Are you feeling sick? Don't eat your lunch if you don't want it.'

'I'm perfectly all right, thanks,' said Tony, untruthfully, and shovelled peas into his mouth. 'Don't bother me, please! I hate being fussed. There's nothing wrong at all!'

14

Greta and Pam

Mrs Farrell might have been more inquisitive about Tony's looks if other things had not claimed her attention just then. Pam was worrying her very much. She was irritable, nervy and impatient. The play was the very next day, and Pam was getting all worked up about it.

She was still cold to her father, and even turned her head away when he kissed her goodnight. She no longer did the loving little things for him that she had always done. She no longer ruffled his greying, curly hair or sat on the arm of his chair. She was an unkind, sulky, unforgiving girl, and her father was unhappy and grieved about it.

But he put it all down to the play and her double work on that and the scholarship. Afterwards surely she would be her own self again! But how could she be so hard and bitter to him, day after day? He was sadly disappointed in his much-loved eldest daughter and turned to quiet little Lizzie for comfort and love.

Lizzie was different these days, he thought. She had always been a kind, loving child, keeping herself too much in the background, scared of people and things. But now she seemed more confident, she looked people straight in the face, she carried herself well and looked as if she had a happy secret. Lizzie noticed that Pam was still cold and unkind to her father and sensed how much it grieved him. She tried to make up to him for Pam's behaviour by running errands for him, and bringing him a special buttonhole in the mornings.

'You're a nice child, Lizzie,' her father said. 'It's about time you went to the oculist again, I think, you may be able to stop wearing those glasses, and I'll take you to the dentist too. Those front teeth of yours seem to be getting properly into place now.'

'Oh good, Daddy!' said Lizzie. 'I'll be so glad to get rid of that wire round them and it will be such a relief not to have to wear my glasses!'

'You'll look a different child without them!' said Aunt Grace. 'John, don't you think our Lizzie's getting quite good-looking lately?'

Lizzie blushed. Mr Farrell laughed and looked closely at her. Yes, Lizzie had a kind of bloom on her. She looked a happy, contented person; not a bit like discontented little Pam, whose mouth was growing hard and ugly.

'I hope Lizzie's glasses and wire will go before

I depart,' said Aunt Grace. 'I'd like to see her without them!'

'Oh, Aunt Grace – are you going?' said Lizzie, in surprise. 'Oh, I wish you'd stay on. Don't go yet.'

'My dear, I've already stayed longer than I should, and said more than I ought, and made myself a worse nuisance than usual!' said Aunt Grace, poking some sunflower seeds through the wires of Sukie's cage. 'As soon as the summer holidays are here I'm going to your Aunt Dora's.'

Good riddance too, thought Pam, coming by on her way out. Interfering old thing. She saw her father and looked the other way. He caught her arm jokingly and swung her round to make her smile at him.

'Don't, Daddy,' she said coldly. 'You'll mess my dress.'

He let her go, his eyes sad. Pam went out and did not even say goodbye.

'What that girl wants . . .' began Aunt Grace, fiercely, but Mr Farrell interrupted her.

'Wait till the play's over,' he said. 'She's all wound up. She'll be all right afterwards.'

Aunt Grace did one of her snorts. Tony could copy these to perfection – but Tony was not doing anything of the sort just then. Nobody could get a word or a laugh out of him. David and Delia avoided him. They were ashamed of him, and afraid of what might happen to him when the whole story came out, as surely it must do!

That evening trouble blew up between Greta and Pam. It had been brewing for some time, for Pam vented her nerviness and irritability on Greta more than on anyone else. She snapped at her. She found fault with her. She left her bedroom in such a mess that at last Greta refused to tidy it.

Pam had wanted a blouse ironed. She had thrown it on a chair and it had slipped to the floor, getting very creased. She had gone to the kitchen with it and had flung it down there.

'Iron this, Greta,' she said. 'I want to wear it tomorrow. It's all creased.'

'No wonder!' said Greta. 'You never hang up your things, never.'

'Don't find fault with me,' snapped Pam. 'I didn't ask you for your opinions. And for heaven's sake don't scorch the blouse.'

'I have no time to iron it,' said Greta, in an obstinate voice. 'Tonight I have much to do, much, much, much. I cannot iron blouses.'

'You're only mending the twins' socks!' said Pam, in a rage. 'Leave those and do something for me for a change. You always make such a fuss when I ask you to do something.'

'You do not ask me. You order me,' said Greta, threading a needle with darning wool. 'I do not like that. I will do anything for anyone if they ask me – but me, I will not be ordered like a dog. Lie down! Iron my blouse! Keep to heel! Tidy my room!'

This sounded comical, but Pam saw nothing funny in it at all. She lost her temper. She banged on the table and shouted.

'You're an insolent creature! I don't know why Mother keeps you. If I had my way I'd send you packing tomorrow. You're disobliging and rude and – and . . .'

Then Greta lost her temper too. She flung down the sock she was mending and leaped to her feet. Her plump, rosy face seemed to swell up with rage.

'Ah, you bad, bad girl!' she hissed. 'So proud, so vain, so cruel! How I hate you! You will give me an apology for your wicked words, or I GO!'

'Well, go!' shouted Pam, beside herself. 'Go, and jolly good riddance to you. I'll tell Mother at once of your rudeness.'

Half crying, she turned to go. But Greta caught hold of her arm. 'You will give me an apology, yes?' she demanded. 'I forgive you, if you are sorry. You are nothing but a spoilt child. If you do not give me the apology, I go.'

'What! Apologise to you! You must be mad!'

144

cried Pam and shook off Greta's hand. 'Don't
dare touch me. You pack and go!'

The girl rushed out of the room and poured
everything out to her mother and her great-
aunt, making out that Greta had been insolent
and had refused to do anything for her, and had
called her wicked names. Mrs Farrell was very
much distressed.

'Oh, Pam dear, I really can't believe that Greta would behave like that.' Hardly had she finished the sentence than the door opened and Greta herself came in. She had on her outdoor clothes.

'Madame,' she said to Mrs Farrell, 'I have to leave you. Not one night more can I sleep under the same roof as this bad girl!'

'Come, Greta!' said Mrs Farrell, 'you mustn't say things like that. Miss Pamela is not a bad girl and you know it.'

'She is bad, very bad, she is hard and cruel and vain,' asserted Greta, quite carried away by her feelings. 'Ah, you are kind, Madame, and Lizzie is like you and the twins, they, they . . .'

'Mother, for goodness' sake let her go,' cried Pam. 'How can you put up with her? Mother, if you don't make her go, I'll – I'll run away!'

'Nonsense, child!' said Aunt Grace, briskly. 'Storm in a teacup, that's what this is. Go and wash your face, Pam. Greta, take off your things and be sensible. You ought to know better than to take Pamela seriously, just when she is over-anxious about the play she's in.'

'It's nothing to do with the play, Madame,' answered Greta. 'She's always like that to me. I've done my best, but tonight I must go. I will send someone for my box tomorrow. Good-night, Madame, goodnight to you both.'

'Greta! You can't leave like this!' cried Mrs

Farrell. 'You can't. You've no right to. You have to give me notice.'

'Madame, I will pay you money if it is not right for me to go,' said Greta, her mouth quivering. 'But I must go. This girl, she makes me very unhappy.'

'Let her go, Mother, let her go!' cried Pam, and would have pushed Greta out of the room herself if her great-aunt had not caught sharply hold of her hands.

Greta went out of the room. Almost at once there came the sound of the kitchen door shutting. Then Greta came into sight of the window, going steadily towards the gate, a small suitcase in her hand. Mrs Farrell sat silent, wondering how in the world the household was going to manage without Greta!

'A fine pickle you've put us into now, with your tantrums, Pam,' said Aunt Grace, picking up her knitting. 'Well, well, you won't be so pleased with yourself when you find you've got to turn to and help in the house now Greta's gone. Your mother and I can't do everything ourselves.'

'We can easily get somebody else,' said Pam, sulkily. 'And Mrs Holloway, the woman who comes in the mornings, can easily come all day. We're well rid of Greta.'

'We're not,' said Aunt Grace, in a sharp tone.

'Greta was a good and kind girl, hard-working and sensible. What the twins will say I don't know!'

The twins said a tremendous lot when they heard what had happened. Greta gone; gone without even saying goodbye to them! They stared at one another in consternation.

'But, Mummy, she'll come back, won't she?' said Delia. 'Mummy, we can't do without her. I did so like her. So did David. Mummy, she simply must come back!'

'Where's she gone?' demanded David. 'I'll go and fetch her back. I'm sure she'll come if Delia and I go for her and carry her bag.'

Mr Farrell was annoyed and upset when he heard the news. He was very fond of Greta. 'She was really one of the family!' he said. 'What a pity you upset her, Pam. She was such a good sort.'

'Yes, you take anybody's part against me,' flared up Pam. 'Anybody's. I'm always the one in the wrong. I'm . . .'

'That will do, Pam,' said Mr Farrell. 'Go to bed early tonight – you're overtired. Thank goodness this play will be over soon. I don't want to see you looking pale and plain as the princess tomorrow.'

'I don't want you to come,' said Pam, standing up. 'I'd rather you didn't come, Daddy. So don't!' She went out of the room, leaving a silence behind her. Mr Farrell sighed. What had come over Pam? She didn't seem like his child any more. She sounded almost as if she couldn't bear him at all.

'Don't take any notice of the silly child,' said Aunt Grace, grieved to see her nephew's face. 'Come to the play and clap her. She'll soon recover!'

'No, I don't think I'll go,' said Mr Farrell. 'She might act better if I'm not there. Poor little Pam, she must be terribly overtired.'

Aunt Grace's needles flew in and out and her thoughts flew with them: Overtired? Not a bit of it! Just a sulky, naughty little schoolgirl who wants a good lesson – and probably won't get it! If she was ten years younger I'd go up and spank her myself!

15

The Day of the Play

The Farrell family was not very happy that night. The grown-ups were sad about Greta going so suddenly. Pam was angry and resentful. Tony was so full of his own worries that he hardly noticed Greta was gone. Lizzie was miserable because people seemed to be so cross and unhappy. Where had all the old fun and laughter and the old love and happiness gone to? Even the twins were down in the dumps. They cast disgusted glances at Tony and did not speak to him, and turned away when Pam appeared.

What's the matter with everyone? thought Lizzie, puzzled. We've all got across one another, we're not pulling together a bit. We might be enemies, not members of one small family. Even I am keeping something from them. I can't tell them my lovely secret because I don't think they'll share my delight in the right way – except perhaps Daddy and the twins. It's horrid!

The next day came. Neither Pam nor Tony had slept much, Pam because she was thinking about the play and Tony because he had worried about little Tom Walters. Both of them looked white and what Aunt Grace called 'peaked'.

Something is wrong with Tony, she thought. I've never known him so quiet. He hasn't cracked a single joke, and he didn't laugh even when Sukie got muddled at breakfast-time and screeched 'hip-hip-hanky' instead of 'hip-hip-hooray'.

It had been strange to be without Greta that morning. Lizzie had got up early and done Greta's work. Mrs Farrell and Aunt Grace had cooked the breakfast. The twins had laid the table. Neither Pam nor Tony had appeared till the gong was sounded. They both muttered good morning and sat down without even a smile for their mother.

Mrs Farrell began talking about plans for the day. 'You'll stay to lunch at school today, Pam dear,' she said. 'And you too, Tony. The twins can come home and Lizzie too, because she'll help me. We'll all be in good time to see your play, Pam, not David and Tony, of course, they'll be at school, but the rest of us. You will come, won't you, John?'

'No. I shan't be there,' said Mr Farrell's voice from behind the newspaper. Lizzie nudged Pam violently.

'Tell Daddy to come, Pam,' she hissed. 'Go on. Tell him!'

But Pam wouldn't. She scowled at Lizzie and dug the spoon hard into the marmalade. Lizzie wondered how anyone could be so hard-hearted towards such a nice father as theirs. Really, Pam was odd.

All the children went off to school. Mrs Holloway, the daily woman, came, and Mrs Farrell went to tell her that Greta had left and to ask her if she could come in more often until they got somebody else. Someone came for Greta's box. It was sad to see it carried out of the gate. Sukie the parrot squawked for her sunflower seeds and Aunt Grace hurried to give her them. Mr Farrell went out to his car, said a word or two to old Frost, and started up his engine.

'Lucy, I'm going!' he called. Usually Mrs Farrell came out to kiss him goodbye, but she was talking to Mrs Holloway and didn't come. Aunt Grace saw her nephew sitting in the car, looking so gloomy that she felt sorry for him. She went to the car window.

'Cheer up, John dear!' she said. 'All families get black patches! Cheer up, my boy, and lose yourself in your splendid work.'

She gave him a kiss and a pat, and he smiled. 'You're the nicest old lady I ever knew!' he said, and off went the car down the drive.

The morning flew by at House at the Corner. There was so much to do without Greta there!

It seemed no time at all till the twins came home to their lunch and Lizzie followed soon after.

'Everyone's getting excited about the play!' she said. 'I don't think there will be an empty seat, Mummy. Daddy will come, won't he? Do make him, Mummy. I'm sure he wants to.'

'I'll see if he will,' said Mrs Farrell. 'It's so silly, the way Pam has behaved to him lately. Now, you serve the vegetables, Lizzie dear. Twins, have you washed? You don't look as if you have.'

'Mum, of course we have,' said David. 'You always think we haven't. Oh good – marrow. Give me lots, Lizzie!'

They began their lunch. Mrs Farrell looked at the clock. 'Daddy's awfully late today! I suppose he has got hung up on some case. Lizzie, put meat and vegetables on a plate for him and pop it into the oven to keep warm.'

They finished their lunch. Still there was no sign of Mr Farrell. 'Oh dear,' said Mrs Farrell, 'his lunch will taste horrid. It's time for us to go and get ready to go to Pam's play, too. What a pity Greta isn't here to see to John when he comes. Mrs Holloway has gone. There won't be anyone here to see to him.'

'I'll do that,' said Aunt Grace, briskly. 'You go up and change into your pretty new dress, Lucy. I'll wait here for John. We can't leave the house empty, with no one to give him his lunch or to answer the telephone. You know that.'

'No. I suppose we can't,' said Mrs Farrell. 'But I did want you to see the play, Aunt Grace, I'm sure Pam will be quite the star of the afternoon!'

Aunt Grace was not sure that she wanted to see Pam shining like a star! She was feeling very much annoyed with her. That naughty girl had upset the whole household and now was going to queen it over everyone that afternoon, getting praise and applause the whole time. No, definitely Aunt Grace didn't wish to join in. She would much rather stay at home and see to poor hungry John!

Mrs Farrell changed into her new dress, saw that Lizzie and Delia looked nice, and set off. It was a glorious afternoon, which was very lucky, for the play was to be in the school grounds. Aunt Grace turned down the gas in the oven, cleared away, washed up and then sat down to her knitting. 'Click, click, click,' said Sukie, copying the sound of the needles.

At three o'clock or just after, the telephone bell rang shrilly. Aunt Grace had dropped off into a doze and it woke her with a start. She dropped her knitting, picked it up carefully, and went to the telephone. It's John saying he can't

get back to lunch after all, she thought. So like the dear boy to ring up long after the time!

'Hello,' said a voice. 'Is that Rivers-End 0012?'

'Yes,' said Aunt Grace. 'Who is speaking?'

'Is that Mrs Farrell?' asked the voice.

'No. She's out,' said Aunt Grace. 'But this is Mr Farrell's aunt speaking. I can take a message for his wife.'

There was a pause. Then the voice went on. 'This is Dr Ellis speaking. I'm afraid I have rather bad news for you.'

Aunt Grace's heart went cold. Bad news? What did that mean?

'What is it?' she asked, almost in a whisper.

'Er – Mr Farrell has had a car accident,' said the voice. 'A lorry ran into him. I'm afraid he's rather badly hurt.'

'Tell me the worst, please,' said Aunt Grace, in a trembling voice. 'I'd rather know.'

'That is the worst,' said the voice. 'He's unconscious. His right arm is broken, and his right hand is badly injured. But he'll come round all right, though it will be some time before his hand is right. He's in Hallerton Hospital. Perhaps you would tell his wife and she can come over. I'm so sorry, so very sorry. Such a fine man – and a most brilliant surgeon.'

Aunt Grace put back the receiver and sank into a chair. 'His right hand!' she said, and a tear ran down her cheek. 'The hand that holds all his skill and power – the hand he operates with, to bring back health and strength to poor wretched people! Why couldn't it have been his left hand?'

She looked for her handkerchief, but as usual she had left it somewhere. She went blindly to find it, rubbing away the tears with her hand. 'Poor John! Poor John! God grant he will be able to use his right hand again. What would he do without the work he loves and lives for? If ever there was a born surgeon, he's one. Poor John!'

She found her handkerchief and wiped her eyes. What should she do now? She must send a message to the school because Mrs Farrell must come at once. Poor Lucy! Oh dear, what a dreadful thing to happen.

With a trembling hand she picked the receiver up and got on to the school. 'I have an urgent message for a Mrs Farrell, who is watching the school play,' she said. 'Could you please tell her there is bad news and she must come home at once?'

'Yes, madam, certainly,' said the school secretary, and the receiver clicked as she put it down. The woman made her way out to the school grounds. She met a mistress taking a child indoors who felt sick. She gave her the message, took the child herself and left the mistress to deliver the message.

Miss Thomas, the mistress, knew Mrs Farrell well. Yes, there she was, sitting at the end of a row, wrapped up in Pam's performance. Pam had just come on, in one of her beautiful, trailing dresses, looking too lovely for words. Her clear little voice sounded over the rustling of the little breeze.

'I pray you, gentlemen, do not hinder me in my good purpose,' she was saying. The girls who were in the audience watching sighed with pleasure. Pam Farrell was so lovely! The grown-ups thought how clever and pretty she was, and Mrs Farrell felt so proud that she could hardly contain herself. What a pity John wasn't there, beside her. He would have been so proud to see Pam's success.

A hand touched her on the shoulder. She turned, to see Miss Thomas's grave face. 'Mrs Farrell, I'm so very sorry, but a message has come to ask you to return home at once. I'm afraid there may be some bad news for you.'

Mrs Farrell's heart almost stopped. Was anything wrong with Tony or David – perhaps it was Aunt Grace? If only John was with her, to help her.

She rose up, looking rather pale. She forgot about Lizzie and Delia. 'What is it, Mummy?' whispered Lizzie, but Mrs Farrell did not hear her. Lizzie wondered what to do. She had vaguely caught the words 'bad news' and she was scared. She forgot about Pam, but sat staring in front of her, puzzled and frightened.

Pam had seen her mother go out and felt annoyed. Now, why did Mother go out like that in the middle, disturbing everybody? And now there was Lizzie rushing out! Whatever was the matter with them? Just as she was coming to her nicest part, too, where she did a little stately dance with the prince!

Lizzie couldn't stay. She simply had to go

after her mother. Delia, left alone, looked round in alarm. Where had Mummy and Lizzie gone? What was the matter?

'Something's happened to David!' said Delia to herself. 'That's what it is! Oh dear, what can it be? I can't stay here alone. I don't want to watch Pam in her old play if anything's wrong with David!'

So, to Pam's intense annoyance she saw Delia too get up and go out. Now there was not one single member of her family to see her triumph! Angry, and a little alarmed too, Pam forgot her lines and had to be prompted. That upset her and soon she forgot again. Miss Romula frowned. Surely Pam was not going to spoil the play by forgetting, when she knew the words so well!

They've spoilt the play for me, thought Pam, trying to smile sweetly at the prince. What a horrid family I've got! They would go and spoil this afternoon for me too.

16

A Black Patch

Meantime Mrs Farrell, Lizzie and Delia were just arriving home. Aunt Grace met them at the gate. Mrs Farrell ran to her. 'What's happened?' she cried. 'Quick, tell me, Aunt Grace.'

'It's John,' said Aunt Grace. 'He's had an accident but he'll be all right, my dear, so don't look like that. I've ordered a car and it'll be round in a minute. We'll go straight to the hospital and see him. Now cheer up – it might be a lot worse!'

The car came round the corner at that moment. Lizzie and Delia, white-faced, went to the car door too. 'No, you can't come,' said Aunt Grace. 'Only your mother. We'll be back as soon as we can. You get tea at half past four, Lizzie dear, and see to things for us. Don't worry now. Daddy will be all right. He's not dangerously hurt.'

The car went off. Delia flung herself on Lizzie, sobbing. 'Daddy's hurt, he's hurt!' she said. 'Poor darling Daddy. That's why he didn't come in to lunch – and we didn't know. Lizzie, I want David.'

'He'll soon be home,' said Lizzie, tears running down her cheeks too. Poor Daddy! She couldn't believe it. Daddy wouldn't come up the drive that evening, driving his car to the garage. He wouldn't sit there at suppertime and ask them all what they had been doing that day. 'Come and tell Greta,' she said, longing for the comfort of the kindly Austrian. Then she remembered that Greta had gone. She and Delia clung to each other for a moment, quite desolate. 'I want David,' sobbed Delia. 'I do want David.'

David came home before Tony, full of news for Delia. He didn't notice at first that Delia's eyes were red. 'I say,' he said, in a worried voice, 'I'm afraid poor old Tony's going to get into a frightful row. The head's come back – and Tony's getting into an awful stew. The head had Blinky and Mr Lehman in his study all afternoon.'

'David – Daddy's had an accident,' burst out Delia. 'Oh, I'm glad you've come back. Come up the garden to our secret place.'

Lizzie watched the twins go off, their arms round each other. They would comfort one another. She began to busy herself with tea preparations. She simply must do something. If only there was somebody else in the house. Greta would have been such a comfort.

Tony came home, looking gloomier than ever. The boys had sent him to Coventry. They came round gladly enough when things went well and he made them laugh, but now he was getting into trouble they turned their backs on him. And what would happen after the meeting of the head, Blinky and Mr Lehman? They were putting two and two together – and soon he, Tony, would be hauled out and required to give an explanation of that awful smell.

Lizzie told him about his father. Tony was struck dumb. His own troubles left his mind for a minute. Dad hurt! How terrible. He plied Lizzie with questions and then went up to his room, sick and anxious. Now Dad wouldn't be able to speak to him, wouldn't be able to stand up for him if he got into serious trouble. Worse than that, had brought trouble on the family just when they couldn't bear any more!

Then Pam arrived, flushed with triumph, but annoyed with herself for not doing as well as she had hoped. Fancy forgetting her words on the day of the play itself! Well, it was Mother's fault, and Lizzie and Delia's, for walking out like that.

'Lizzie!' she called, when she saw her sister. 'Why did you all go out? You put me off and I forgot my words!'

Lizzie turned a tear-stained face to her sister.

'Pam, Daddy's had a car accident,' she said.
'Mummy got the message during the play and
she went out. Delia and I were so worried we
simply had to go too, and find out.'

Pam stared. Daddy in an accident! She went
pale and sat down suddenly. 'Tell me about it,'
she said, in an odd little voice. 'Quick, tell me.'

Lizzie told her. She went and put her arms
round Pam. 'It's awful, isn't it?' she said. 'Poor
dear old Daddy.'

'It's more awful for me than anyone!' cried
Pam, suddenly, in a high, unnatural voice, and
she pushed Lizzie away. 'I wouldn't kiss him

goodbye this morning! I told him not to come to my play. But I d-d-d-d-didn't know this was going to happen. Oh Daddy, I'm sorry, I'm so sorry!' Lizzie had never seen Pam so distressed. She tried to put her arms round her again but Pam would not have it. 'Don't touch me!' she cried. 'I'm wicked! This is a punishment for me for being so mean to Daddy!'

'Oh, Pam, that's nonsense,' said Lizzie, sturdily. 'Daddy's accident would have happened whether you had been mean to him or not.'

'It wouldn't, it wouldn't,' said Pam, choking. 'If I'd asked him to come to my play – as you wanted me to at breakfast-time – he'd have been home in good time for lunch – and the accident wouldn't have happened. I know it wouldn't.'

Lizzie gazed at her sister despairingly. She didn't know what to say. If Aunt Grace was here she would know how best to deal with poor Pam, but Lizzie had no idea. Pam, still weeping, went up to her room and threw herself on her bed. She did not stop to think that she might have helped Lizzie to prepare tea. She was unhappy and that was all that mattered.

It was a very sorrowful little household that gathered together for a late tea. Mrs Farrell had stayed behind at the hospital. Mr Farrell was conscious again, but in pain, and he wanted his wife near him. She sat by him, reproaching herself bitterly for not having gone out to say goodbye to him properly that morning. Such little things – and what big things they became when it was too late.

'You went and kissed him goodbye,' wept Mrs Farrell to Aunt Grace. 'I didn't bother.'

'That doesn't matter at all,' said Aunt Grace, in a comforting, matter-of-fact voice. 'You were talking to Mrs Holloway. For goodness' sake, Lucy, don't fret yourself with little things like that when there are so many bigger things to worry about!'

She went back to the children, leaving their mother behind at the hospital. The five Farrells clustered round her as soon as she appeared, feeling glad to see a responsible grown-up with them at last!

'Well, my dears, your father's not unconscious any more,' said Aunt Grace. 'He'll be all right. His right arm is broken, but that will soon mend.'

'Was he hurt anywhere else?' asked Lizzie, anxiously.

Aunt Grace hesitated. The gravest thing of all was the injury to their father's right hand, which might make it impossible for him ever to use it again for anything skilful or deft, such as surgery. And surgery was his work, his job. What would he do if he couldn't practise his profession? It would be a terrible thing for him. Aunt Grace could not make up her mind whether or not to tell the children.

'Aunt Grace – you're keeping something from us!' said Pam, suddenly. 'You are, I know you are. What is it? You've got to tell us.'

'Well, I will,' said Aunt Grace. 'His right hand is badly injured. You will know what that means to him.'

There was a silence. Then Delia's voice was lifted in a wail. 'Oh Aunt Grace! Daddy will be miserable!'

Tony was shocked. 'But Aunt Grace, won't he ever be able to, to – to do operations again?' he stammered. 'What will he do, then?'

'We won't cross our bridges before we come to them,' said Aunt Grace. 'Things may be better than they seem to be at the moment. I'm dying for a cup of tea. Lizzie, is the kettle boiling?'

'Yes, Aunt Grace,' said Lizzie, glad to turn her tear-stained face away for a moment. 'I'll get it.'

'I don't want any tea,' said Pam. 'It would choke me. Aunt Grace, it doesn't seem real – it doesn't seem true. I feel so dreadful because I – because I . . .'

'Yes. I can guess how you feel,' said Aunt Grace, in a gentle voice. 'Remorse is a terrible thing to bear, Pam, one of the worst of all punishments in this life. To wish undone something you have done, to wish you could look back on kindness to someone you love, instead of on unkindness, that is a very terrible thing.'

Pam felt desperately unhappy. Life was very black indeed. If only she had asked Daddy to come to her play! Pam felt certain that it was because of her unkindness that her father had met with his accident. She couldn't forgive herself. 'And I never shall forgive myself!' she said. 'Never! I didn't know I was so wicked till today. Now I do know. Whatever shall I do?'

The twins decided to go out and do some gardening. Aunt Grace approved. 'Better to do some hard work when trouble happens along,' she said. 'Hard work is always a help. You go out and garden too, Pam.'

'I couldn't,' said Pam. 'I can't do anything. I can't.'

Aunt Grace left her to herself. Poor Pam, so wrapped up in her own feelings. Nobody could do anything for her. She would have to pull herself together sooner or later. Good little Delia and David – weeding away furiously in the drive – and Lizzie cooking something in the kitchen. Tony was nowhere to be seen. What was the matter with that boy? Aunt Grace did hope he wasn't going to be ill. There was trouble enough already at House at the Corner, without any more coming!

Mrs Farrell did not come home that night, but telephoned to say that her husband was no worse, and she would stay with him that night. Aunt Grace spoke to her cheerfully.

'Now don't you worry about anything, Lucy. I'm here and I can look after the children as well as you can. We're managing very well. Lizzie, as usual, is being a little brick, and the twins are slaving away in the garden. Don't you worry about anything!'

'I don't know what I should do without you, Aunt Grace,' said Mrs Farrell. 'You won't go off to Dora's, will you, now this has happened? You'll stay on for the holidays, won't you? – till we see how John does. Don't desert me!'

'Of course not, Lucy!' said Aunt Grace. 'I shall be only too glad to stay on and help. With Greta gone, I can do quite a bit for you.'

Aunt Grace bustled round, her heart sad but her face as cheerful as she could make it. Mrs Farrell would have to be at the hospital a good deal for the next week. Greta was gone. Mrs Holloway couldn't give them very much extra time. So she and the children would have to bestir themselves if they were going to keep the house clean and tidy, and everything going as usual.

Everyone must have his or her job. Yes, even that lazy little Pam. Do her good to turn to for a bit! If she was as sorry about things as she said she was, then she must show it by really helping. She suddenly remembered the little boy, Tom Walters, who had been so badly hurt the day before. She wondered how he was getting on.

She called to David. 'David! How is Tom? Have you heard?'

Tony, up in his bedroom, heard David's clear voice from the garden, answering Aunt Grace who stood at the side door. 'Oh, he's a bit better today, Aunt Grace. Our form master told us. We're taking him flowers tomorrow, and I'm going to give him my book on butterflies and moths. He's mad on those. Delia's sending him her book on birds.'

Tony listened. He felt weighed down with misery and anxiety. Dad in hospital – little Tom hurt because of his foolish prank – all the boys cold-shouldering him – even David not speaking a word to him! He heard David's voice again. 'Tom's father is furious about it. He's seeing the head tonight.'

A picture of the stern Mr Walters flashed into Tony's mind. He groaned. Things were going from bad to worse.

17

Saturday Morning

The next day was Saturday. Mrs Farrell had slept at the hospital in order to be near her husband, and it seemed very strange to everyone not to see either their mother or father at the breakfast table. Lizzie and Aunt Grace had got breakfast between them. Pam still seemed too distressed to do anything at all. She wept without ceasing, and her face no longer had any prettiness left in it.

'Pull yourself together, child,' said Aunt Grace a little sharply. 'What good are you doing to anyone, crying like that? You certainly are not helping your father. He would be most upset if he saw you like this.'

'You don't understand, Aunt Grace, you don't understand,' wept Pam. 'I made Daddy have his accident. If I hadn't been so mean, if I'd asked him to come to the play, he wouldn't have – he wouldn't have had – his accident. And, oh, I wouldn't even say goodbye that morning. I keep on and on thinking about it, I can't forget it, I can't forgive myself, I feel so wicked, so very wicked . . .'

'Well, I think you're being rather silly,' said Aunt Grace. 'I can understand your being very, very sorry for your unkindness, I thought you were a selfish and unkind daughter, I must say, but I did think you would have a little more strength of character, and wouldn't give way so completely like this.'

'I made Daddy think I didn't love him,' said Pam, beginning to weep all over again. 'But I do. I'm more upset than anyone about this accident. I couldn't possibly eat a big breakfast like the twins or set about housework like Lizzie. I feel much too upset.'

That was too much for Lizzie. She stood up fiercely. 'Pam! I feel as bad as you, and worse, about Daddy but I've got a bit more control over myself and my feelings, thank goodness. And how could I possibly leave Aunt Grace to do everything while I sat about and wept? I want to howl every time I think about Daddy's poor hand – but I can't just think of my own feelings when there are the twins to see to, and so many things to do. Why can't *you* help? What about the weekend shopping? Can't you go and do it?'

'What! With my eyes all swollen and face all red?' cried Pam. 'You're hard and unkind, Lizzie.'

'There's the telephone,' said Aunt Grace,

172

thankful to hear the bell ringing. 'Answer it, Lizzie dear.'

It was someone to inquire after Mr Farrell. It was one of the many many calls from his scores of friends, for he was a much-loved man. Lizzie was full of deep joy to know how much respected and loved her father was. She wrote down all the messages to give to her mother when she next saw her.

The twins went to clean out the hen-run and hen-house. They did this every Saturday. Old Frost was there waiting for them. 'I'm that sorry to hear about your pa,' he said to them. 'A fine gennelman he is, a proper man. You tell me when you can go and see him and I'll bring you the best roses out of my cottage garden for him. And looky here – my old woman has made these for you two.' He handed the twins a paper bag. Inside were two large-sized jam tarts. Delia and David were touched. Dear old Mrs Frost, it was her way of telling them she was sorry for their trouble – two big jam tarts!

'It's awfully decent of Mrs Frost,' said David, beginning to eat his tart. 'She does make such nice tarts. We'll call in and thank her this evening, Mr Frost.'

'Yes, we will,' said Delia. 'And we'll take your roses when we go to see Daddy. You know, Mr Frost, he's hurt his right hand very much.'

Frost leaned on his fork. 'Ah, that's bad,' he said. 'That's real bad. What's he going to do if he can't use it? His job will be done! Ah, it's a bad thing when a man can't do his work.'

The twins nodded solemnly. The fact that their father might not be able to carry on with his work was worrying them very much.

'It's a pity we're only ten,' said Delia, as they methodically raked the droppings out of the hen-house. 'We could easily leave school and go to work then, to help Daddy.'

'Yes, we could. We could do jobs in anyone's gardens,' said David. 'We can grow just as good vegetables as Mr Frost can. If we were eighteen, like Pam, or sixteen like Lizzie, we could easily leave school and work. I should like that. Or even if we were fourteen like Tony, we could find a job.'

'Pooh – Tony wouldn't be any good at any

job,' said Delia, putting the droppings into a tin bath. 'Help me to carry this to the compost heap, Dave. Catch hold. You see, Tony's not trustable, is he? He'd just fool around, whatever job he got.'

'I think Daddy always hoped Tony might be a doctor too,' said David, helping Delia to carry the tin bath. 'I think he's disappointed that Tony won't follow him in his job.'

There was a minute's silence as the twins emptied the bath on to the big compost heap, raked it, and threw a layer of old leaves over the droppings to hide the smell. They always did everything very thoroughly.

'Delia,' said David, thoughtfully, 'do you think *we* ought to make up our minds to be doctors, so as not to disappoint Daddy?'

'I thought we'd made up our minds to be farmers, and have a farm together,' said Delia, in a disappointed voice. 'I don't think I'd like the messing about in people's insides. But I will, if you want to.'

'No, I don't want to,' said David. 'Come on, let's put some peat-moss on the hen-house floor. I want a farm with you more than anything in the world. Only I feel so sorry about Daddy now that I just thought if it would make him happy I'd tell him we'd be doctors.'

'All right,' said Delia, and heaved a sigh. 'We

can't all disappoint Daddy. Pam's awful. Tony's an idiot, the way he behaves. Lizzie's nice, but she never does anything to make Daddy or Mummy proud of her. So I suppose we'd better do our bit.'

'We'll ask Michael,' said David. 'He'll know.'

'We ought to ask Michael about Pam, too,' said Delia. 'I heard Aunt Grace say that poor Pam was sick in her soul. Perhaps Michael would know what to do about it. He's going to be a mender of souls. He could try himself out on Pam!'

'Don't you say that to Pam!' said David. 'She'd be furious. Why doesn't she stop howling and help? She's just as lazy and selfish as ever. That's enough peat-moss, Delia. Now let's mend that hole in the wire.'

Talking seriously to one another, as they always did, the twins got on with their jobs. No one but Frost knew how much they did in the garden. They loved it. They both had what Frost called 'green thumbs' and could make anything grow in a most miraculous way.

The telephone kept ringing every now and again. The twins heard it as they worked, and guessed it was people ringing up about their father. They wished their mother would come home. Without either of their parents the house didn't seem like home.

'There goes the telephone again,' said Delia. 'Poor old Lizzie must be tired of answering it!'

'Hello!' Lizzie was saying. 'Yes, this is Mr Farrell's house. Oh – you want Tony! I'll just go and find him. One minute please.'

She went to find her brother. He was not in the playroom. She called him. 'Tony! Tony! You're wanted on the telephone.'

'I can't come!' shouted Tony from upstairs. 'I'm busy. I expect it's only Rawlings. I don't want to talk to him.'

'It didn't sound like Rawlings,' said Lizzie. She picked up the telephone again. 'Hello! I'm afraid my brother is busy at the moment. Can I take a message?'

'No,' said the voice, sharply. 'He's to come and take it himself. Get him, please. Tell him it's his headmaster speaking.'

'Oh – yes, I will,' said Lizzie, scared at the sharp voice. She once more shouted upstairs to Tony.

'Tony! You must come! It's your headmaster and he sounded awfully cross.'

Tony's heart went cold and a horrible sinking feeling came into his stomach. He was sitting on his bed and he had to make himself get up. His legs shook under him. The head – that could only mean one thing. They knew he'd got something to do with the accident to Tom Walters.

'Tony! You *must* come!' shouted Lizzie again. 'Hurry up, do.'

Tony got himself downstairs somehow. He went into his father's consulting room and shut the door. He picked up the telephone receiver there.

'Tony Farrell here, sir,' he said, in as bright a voice as he could manage. 'Sorry to have kept you waiting, sir.'

'Farrell, I want you to come to the school this afternoon at half past two,' said the head's voice. 'To my study. Sharp at half past two. Is that clear?'

'Yes, sir,' said Tony, in a small voice, his heart sinking down into his boots.

'I have no doubt that you will guess why I want to see you,' said the head, in a stern voice. Tony hesitated. Should he say yes or no? Should he plunge into a hurried explanation now and hope that would be enough? Or should . . . but it was too late to decide anything, for the head put down his receiver with a click and the telephone went dead.

Tony sat down in a chair, feeling lost and miserable. If his father had been at home he would have gone to him, made a clean breast of everything and begged him to help him. Dad would have known what was best to do. But even Mum wasn't at home. There was Aunt Grace, but she would be so scornful of him and say such sharp things. No, he couldn't tell Aunt Grace. He couldn't tell anyone.

Lizzie opened the door and peeped in. 'Oh, you've finished on the phone. Tony – whatever's the matter? You look awful. Are you ill?'

'No,' said Tony, standing up. 'I'm all right.'

'Why did the head want you?' asked Lizzie. 'He sounded in rather a rage.'

'Don't be so inquisitive,' said Tony and walked out of the room. He pursed up his lips, trying to whistle a tune. But his lips trembled and no sound came. He couldn't even whistle now!

Lizzie stared after him, troubled. It couldn't be just Daddy's accident that made Tony act like that, he had been odd before then. What could it be? She watched him going up the stairs, looking so miserable that her heart was touched.

'Tony!' she called. 'What's up? Do, do tell me. I might help.'

Tony turned round and for a moment was tempted to tell Lizzie everything. Then he turned back again. No – best not to tell anyone. Maybe, once he'd had his telling-off and whatever punishment the head had decided on, everything would blow over, and nobody need know anything at home. He couldn't bear Lizzie or the rest to know that he was in disgrace.

When the gong went for lunch, the twins came hurrying in to wash their dirty hands and faces. Pam came to the table, looking white and miserable, but ready for her lunch. Tony came down too, trying to look the same as usual.

But he could eat hardly anything, for he was worrying so much about seeing the head that afternoon. What would happen to him? Would Mr Walters be there? Tony was very much afraid of him. He tried to eat his meal but he couldn't. He got up, muttered an excuse and went out.

'Let him be,' said Aunt Grace. 'Something's upset him. Perhaps if he rests this afternoon, he'll be all right.'

But there was to be no rest for Tony that afternoon! At a quarter past two he was on his bicycle pedalling gloomily to school. He didn't dare to be even one second late.

18

In the Headmaster's Study

At exactly half past two Tony stood trembling outside his headmaster's study door. From inside came the murmur of voices. To the boy's intense dismay he heard the deep rumble of Mr Walters' voice. He knocked. The head's voice came from inside. 'Come in.'

Tony went in and shut the door. He stood just inside, a big well-built boy, his easy smile no longer on his face. Before him, seated round the head's desk, were four men: the head, grave and stern; Mr Lehman, a scornful look on his thin face; Mr Holmes peering through his glasses, looking very worried indeed; and worst of all, Mr Walters, overwhelming in every way.

'Good afternoon, sir,' faltered Tony, to the head. 'You – you wanted me, sir.'

'We did,' said the head. 'I imagine you know why?'

'Not – not exactly, sir,' said poor Tony, wishing that his knees didn't feel so weak.

'Well, it will be our business this afternoon to let you know exactly and accurately why we want you,' rapped out the head. 'Farrell, did you throw that bottle out of the window and hit young Walters on the head?'

Tony swallowed hard. 'Yes, sir,' he said at last. 'I did throw it, but I didn't know anyone was in the playground, honestly I didn't.'

'It didn't occur to you that it was a dangerous thing to do, to throw a bottle out of the window without even looking to see if anyone was below?' went on the head.

'No, sir,' said Tony. 'I'm very, very sorry.'

'Sorry when it's too late to be sorry!' exploded Mr Walters. 'Sorry when you've landed yourself into trouble! But not sorry about my young Tom. You didn't try to find out how the lad was – you didn't come to tell me what you'd done, and ask if you could do anything for Tom. Pah!'

This was all said very fiercely. Tony went white, and stared speechlessly at the angry man. The head spoke again, gravely and sternly.

'Farrell, your behaviour in this matter is a great disgrace to a family honoured in this district – all of us know and respect your father very highly. It is astounding to us all that he should have a son who is so irresponsible, so cowardly, and so untrustworthy in every way.'

Hot tears pricked at the back of Tony's eyelids. Never in his life had anyone spoken like this to him, never, never had anyone told him he was cowardly.

'Sir . . . sir, I'm not cowardly,' he gulped out.

'And I say you are!' burst out Mr Walters. 'You threw that bottle to get rid of it because you were afraid of being hauled up for that idiotic trick – and then you were too cowardly to own up to being the cause of my Tom's accident, too cowardly even to ask how the lad was!'

Tony couldn't say anything to that. He suddenly saw that he was indeed a coward – all smiles and bravado when things went well, but no pluck or courage to tackle things rightly when they went wrong. Yes, he was a coward.

'Your form master has told me of the stupid trick you played, which led up to the accident,' said the head. 'He has also given me an extremely bad report of your general behaviour and bad influence on the other boys. He adds that you have very good brains indeed, but that you never use them for anything worthwhile at all, only to upset the class and make things easy for yourself and difficult for everyone else. Mr Lehman has also reported fully to me, and I have had reports from other masters who take your form for various lessons. I am afraid, Farrell, that no one has a good word for you.'

'No, sir,' whispered Tony.

'You have had many chances, my boy,' said the head, 'and each time you have thrown them away. Brains are no good without strength of character. You are in your fifteenth year, and so far have wasted most of your schooling. Your parents must be extremely disappointed in you.'

Tony stared desperately at the head. Was he never going to stop saying these terrible things in that awful, stern voice of his?

'Mr Walters wanted to ask your father's permission to punish you,' said the head.

Tony's heart sank further still. He stared in despair at the burly form of Mr Walters. There was a silence for a few moments. Then Mr Walters spoke.

'Yes, that's what I thought I'd do, young Farrell, and that's what you need. But your father did a fine job on my Tom's head, and he's a man I've a great liking for. I hear he's had a bad accident too, poor fellow. He'll feel worse still when he hears about you being the cause of my boy's accident. Extraordinary that such a fine fellow should have a boy like you!'

'Mr Walters was going to punish you for being the stupid cause of his boy's accident,' said the head. 'I *am* going to punish you for your continual bad behaviour, which has such a bad influence on the class you are in. This school, Farrell, has too many boys already, and we are having to pick and choose among them. I intend in future only to keep or to accept those we feel will be a credit to the school. I am afraid I must ask your father to take you away this term. We would rather you did not attend any more.'

Tony could hardly believe his ears. That meant he was being expelled – the biggest disgrace that could befall any boy! He couldn't believe it. No, no – he, Tony Farrell, son of the much-loved doctor; he couldn't be expelled!

'You understand what I am saying, Farrell?' said the head gravely. 'You will not return here next term.'

'Sir – oh sir – don't do that to me!' begged Tony and the tears gushed out down his cheeks.

'I've been a fool and a coward, I know I have. But won't you believe that I'm sorry, I've learned my lesson, I'll never behave like that again? Sir, don't expel me, you don't know what my father will feel like and it will break my mother's heart. Don't do that to me!'

'Farrell, I have other boys to think about besides you,' said the head. 'Other boys who may grow slack and irresponsible and untrustworthy, wasting their time and their brains because of you. You are a bad influence. I am sorry for your parents but I have a duty to the other boys and their parents also. You have had your chance, many chances, and you have wasted them all. Whether another school will take you or not I cannot say, but if your father finds one, then let this be a lesson to you and, in future, use your brains to good purpose, and turn over a new leaf from the first day you go there.'

'Sir, don't send me away from here,' Tony besought the head, almost beside himself with despair. What would his mother say? And Dad! And all the rest of them. And all the town would know – how the boys would sneer!

Mr Holmes suddenly spoke out of the kindness of his heart. 'Sir, perhaps the boy will have learned his lesson now; should we give him one more chance? I don't believe he is really bad at heart.'

Tony could have licked Blinky's boots for those few kind words. But the head was made of harder stuff than kind-hearted Mr Holmes. He shook his head.

'No. The boy must have a hard lesson. It's the only way. Farrell, I shall write to your mother this weekend, as I cannot write to your father.'

'Please, sir, I do beg of you, don't write to my mother yet,' begged Tony. 'She's so upset about my father – she couldn't bear to have this bad news too. Please don't write yet. I'll do anything, anything, if only you won't write and tell her. She's so upset just now.'

'Well,' said the head, and paused. Mr Walters put in a word, speaking very gruffly.

'It'll have a bad effect on Mr Farrell, if Mrs Farrell gets upset just now,' he said. 'I don't want to make things harder for either of them. Mr Farrell was so good about my boy, took no end of trouble over him at the hospital. For his sake we'd better not tell the boy's mother yet.'

'Very well,' said the head. 'Nothing shall be said till things are better with the Farrells. Perhaps, Farrell, you would rather tell your parents yourself, when your father is better?'

Poor Tony! He tried to think which would be better for his parents – hearing the news from him, or having a letter from the head! He thought perhaps it would not be so dreadful for them if they heard it from him, though how he was ever going to break the news to them he didn't know. Life was indeed very black for Tony just then.

'I'll tell them myself,' he said. 'Thank you, sir. I know I deserve my punishment, and I'll take it, and – and learn from it, sir. I'm terribly sorry about young Walters. If Mr Walters would let me I'll go and see him now and tell him I'm sorry. I was in such a muddle and so afraid about everything before that I didn't even dare to ask how he was, but I'd like to go and see him. Oh sir – I'm sorry to have brought all this on the school!'

Poor Tony gave a loud sob, and then, ashamed, tried to turn it into a cough. Mr Holmes looked most uncomfortable. He was intensely sorry for Tony. He had never liked him, but he had a gentle, kindly nature and hated to see any boy in disgrace or unhappy.

'You may go, Farrell,' said the head. 'Learn from this afternoon, and it will not be wasted. Perhaps you will make good after all, and bring honour to your family, instead of disgrace.'

Tony turned and went out. He went to the shed where he had put his bicycle. There was no one there at all. The boy sat down on a wooden bench, put his face in his hands and cried bitterly. He was not only crying for him-self, but for his parents, who would be so

unhappy about him, and for his brother and sisters who would feel his disgrace. He was bringing punishment on them too, as well as on himself.

'I just thought of myself,' wept Tony. 'I didn't think of disappointing others. What am I to do? I'm sure no other school will take me. I shall have to get a job. But I don't know what work I could do. I'm hopeless. I'm a failure. I wish I'd never been born!'

He sat there till he heard the school clock strike half past three. Then he scrubbed his swollen face with his handkerchief and smoothed back his rumpled hair. He'd better go home and wash his face. He'd cycle home by the little lanes, so that no one would see him. Thank goodness the head had promised that he wouldn't write to Mum. That would put off the bad news for a bit. He wouldn't need to let anybody know it all yet.

He got on his bicycle and rode off, a very miserable and ashamed boy. He remembered how he had determined to work hard the next term in Snorter's class. Now he wouldn't have the chance. He would have to go to school for the next few days – then, when they broke up on Thursday, he wouldn't be going any more. It seemed impossible!

He slipped into the house unseen by anyone except Sukie the parrot. She called after him, 'Where's your hanky? Where's your hanky?'

He heard the voices of the twins, still working in the garden. How they slaved out there. He heard somebody down in the kitchen, ironing. *Bump-bump-bump* went the iron. Everything was going on as usual except that Dad and Mum were not there – going on as usual, when his whole life had been changed, and he couldn't see into the future at all!

'What a fool I've been!' said Tony. 'What an unbelievable fool!'

19

Sunday

The news was better that night from the hospital. Mr Farrell was more cheerful and Mrs Farrell was coming home for the night. The children cheered up at once. It would make a difference if their mother was home! Aunt Grace was good and kind and looked after everything well – but nobody was the same as their mother.

Mrs Farrell arrived home late, and the children came round her at once, questioning her, welcoming her back. She had made up her mind that she would be brave with them and talk cheerfully, but their anxious faces and loving hands made the tears come to her eyes. How good to have her children round her again – what fine children they were, Mrs Farrell thought lovingly.

She saw that Tony looked pale and thin-faced, but she thought that it was because he had been worried about his father. She was sad to see Pam's face so altered too; what a shock it had been for them all.

Aunt Grace had had a talk with Pam before her mother had arrived. 'Now you pull yourself together, Pam, when your mother comes,' she said. 'She's upset enough as it is without you having hysterics all over her. Keep your weeping and wailing for when she's at the hospital. If you've got to be weak and feeble like this, don't let her see it.'

Pam thought Aunt Grace very unkind, but she did pull herself together and didn't indulge in too much weeping. They all got quite cheerful over supper, even Tony, who was doing his best not to let his mother guess his unhappiness.

The next day was Sunday. 'I'm going to church,' announced Aunt Grace. 'We cooked the joint last night, and it can be eaten cold today with salad, so that nobody needs to stop at home and see to things if they'd rather go to church. I'm going to get down on my knees and thank God for sparing your father to us – he might easily have been killed!'

'We're going too,' said David. 'It's a good place to go to when you're in trouble. Once, when Delia and I . . .'

'Oh, don't tell about that, Dave,' begged Delia. 'That's private.'

David said no more and the family never knew why Delia and David had once gone solemnly into the village church all by themselves.

'I'm coming,' said Lizzie. 'Mummy, you'll be going to the hospital, won't you? Don't forget

192

to give Daddy our messages, will you, and the book I bought him?'

'And you will give him the raspberries we picked, won't you?' begged Delia. 'He does like them so.'

'I'll give him everything,' promised Mrs Farrell. 'He'll be so pleased to know what a loving family he has.'

Pam had pushed a note into her mother's hand. 'It's very private, for Daddy alone, Mother,' she whispered. 'Just to tell him I'm sorry, and I do love him. And you'll give him the roses, won't you?'

Tony sent him a jigsaw to do. He liked doing those himself when he was ill in bed, and he felt sure his father would like to as well. How he wished he could tell his father some splendid news – that he was going to be moved up in form or was top in exams! But he couldn't.

'I'm coming to church too,' announced Tony, to everyone's surprise. As a rule it was very difficult to get him to go. Pam said nothing. Should she go? She hardly ever did but, as Aunt Grace said, her soul was sick, and perhaps it could be made to feel a little better if she went there, and kneeled down to pour out everything in her prayers. Nobody seemed to listen to her self-reproaches, but God would.

She did not go with the others, but set off by

herself later. She sat right at the back where no one saw her. She felt better as soon as she entered the cool, quiet church, with its old, old smell and its sense of peace.

She had forgotten that prayer could bring comfort and peace. Now she learned it all over again as she kneeled by herself in the back pew. The sunlight came through the old stained-glass windows and made coloured patterns on the stone floor. It was strange how near God always seemed in church, Pam thought. It was a good place to come to when you were in trouble. Delia and David were right.

The Rector came up to the Farrell family after

the service, to speak a few words of sympathy. Delia caught his hand. 'When is Michael coming home?' she asked. 'This week?'

'He's coming back tomorrow,' said the Rector. 'His school is breaking up early because of some repairs that have to be done. He'll be sure to come straight along and see you!'

'Tomorrow!' said David. 'Oh, jolly good. We badly want to talk to him. It's very important.'

The Farrells walked home together. Pam joined them, looking much better. Aunt Grace glanced at her curiously but said nothing. She was glad to know the girl had been to church even though she had not sat with the others.

Jean came round in the afternoon, full of concern about Mr Farrell. She had only heard the news that morning. She was surprised when the door was opened by Lizzie instead of by the beaming Greta.

'Where's Greta?' she asked. 'Is she out? I want to ask her if she'll give me the recipe for that Viennese pudding she makes. Do you think she'd mind?'

'Greta's gone,' said Lizzie. 'Do you want to see Pam? She's in her room, I think.'

'Yes, I'll go up,' said Jean. 'I was upset to hear of your trouble, Lizzie. Mother and I were away for the day yesterday and we only heard this morning. Shall I just leave a note to ask

Greta to write out that recipe for me? You said she'd gone out, didn't you?'

'I said she'd gone – left,' said Lizzie, and looked embarrassed, for she did not like to tell Jean about the row that Greta and Pam had had.

'Gracious!' said Jean, surprised. 'I thought she was quite one of the family. She seemed so fond of you all. What a pity to go just now when you're in trouble.'

'She went before Daddy's accident,' said Lizzie. 'There's Pam calling you, Jean. Go on upstairs.'

Pam, like Lizzie, would not say much to Jean about Greta. She was feeling ashamed of that affair now, and also things were not nearly so comfortable without the hard-working Austrian. Pam wished she had kept her temper. Greta's going had made things harder for the household just when they could have done with the kindness and willingness of the generous-hearted Greta.

'I suppose you have to turn to and do a lot of jobs now, then?' asked Jean, sitting on the window seat.

'Oh, Lizzie does most,' said Pam. 'She likes messing about. I never did. I suppose I shall have to help a bit in the hols. Thank goodness I shall be off to college in September though. Did you know Aunt Grace is staying on now, for most of the hols, anyway – and that horrid parrot?'

'Well, your great-aunt will be a help,' said Jean. 'All five of you will be home, won't you – there'll be a lot to do. You'll really have to help, Pam. It's a pity you've never learned much about cooking and housework. Perhaps I'd better come and give you a few lessons!'

'Oh, we'll soon get someone else,' said Pam, easily. Then her face lengthened. 'Jean, isn't it awful about Daddy? I've never cried so much in my life.'

'Yes. I was terribly sorry,' said Jean. 'I do like your father. Everybody does. He just spends his whole life rushing round giving people back their health and strength. He's a wonder.'

Mrs Farrell came back in time for supper that evening, full of messages for the children from their father. She had a private word with Aunt Grace afterwards.

'It's terrible about his poor hand,' she said, looking strained and anxious. 'The specialist has examined it today. They can save the hand – not take it off, I mean, thank goodness – but they don't think it will ever be any use for his work again. Whatever shall we do, Aunt Grace? All those children to educate and this big house to keep up – and the big garden. We can't do it.'

Aunt Grace was silent. Her knitting-needles

flew in and out. Her thoughts were not with the children but with the injured man. What would he feel like if he could never do his work again? Her heart ached for her nephew. Poor John!

'Of course, Pam can go to college with her scholarship,' said Mrs Farrell. 'So we shan't have much expense with her. Tony can still keep on at his school – it's not so terribly expensive. I'm afraid Lizzie will have to leave, though. Pity she's never been clever enough to win a scholarship! And of course the twins can't go to that expensive boarding-school now. I'm afraid they'll be terribly disappointed.'

'We must have a family council soon,' said Aunt Grace, patting her hair for falling hairpins and pushing one or two back firmly. 'As soon as the holidays begin. If Lizzie has to leave we must warn the head at once, and we must write to Whyteleafe School and tell them we can't afford to send the twins now. A pity that, they would have enjoyed themselves there, together all day long.'

'Perhaps Tony can win a scholarship now,' said Mrs Farrell, brightening up a little. 'He's so clever, Aunt Grace, and I'm sure as soon as he leaves that silly Blinky's form and goes up into a higher class under – what's his name? – I can only think of his nickname, Snorter, I'm sure Tony will work marvellously then. He could easily win a scholarship. That would be a great load off our shoulders.'

'We'll manage, Lucy, don't you worry,' said Aunt Grace. 'Face up to trouble, I always say, and it's wonderful how it melts away. Run away from it and it will swallow you up!'

'You're such a sensible person,' said Mrs Farrell, patting Aunt Grace's hand. 'I don't know what I should have done without you this weekend. You know I'm not very good at facing up to trouble, Aunt Grace, I've always had people to do it for me; first my mother, and then John. They've always tackled trouble for me. I feel a bit lost somehow.'

'Rubbish!' said Aunt Grace, knitting away briskly again. 'If you can't tackle things at your age, my dear, you never will. John will look to you now for a while, and the children will too. We'll manage things all right, you'll see!'

'Have the twins been good?' asked Mrs Farrell. 'I suppose they've been gardening as usual!'

'Good as gold,' said Aunt Grace. 'They're a fine, sturdy pair of characters, Lucy. You still think of them as babies. They're not.'

'They'll probably be as clever as Pam and Tony,' said Mrs Farrell. 'Poor Lizzie, she's so plain and shy and dull, the only one of them that doesn't shine in any way. I don't expect she'll mind leaving school.'

Aunt Grace longed to tell Mrs Farrell about Lizzie – no, not Lizzie – Elizabeth! She longed to tell her how well the girl wrote, and what a fine success she had already had. She longed to show her the stories the girl was having printed week by week. Plain, shy, dull? Why, Lizzie was the best of the lot!

But she had promised Lizzie not to say a word. She and Lizzie shared the secret together, and the girl seemed quite content. She had a fine store of money now, for Aunt Grace changed the cheques every week that came for her. Aunt Grace guessed that generous Lizzie would use it to help the family, now that it looked as if her father would not be able to go on with his professional work – at any rate for some considerable time.

'Lizzie's a fine girl,' said Aunt Grace, clicking her needles loudly. 'Wait till she's got those glasses off and that wire round her teeth, then you won't call her plain! As for having no brains, you wait and see! Mark my words, our Lizzie will give you all a big surprise one day!'

20

A Shock for Pam

Tony went back to school the following day, subdued and very quiet. Mr Holmes was sorry for him, and treated him with gentleness. The other boys, thinking that Tony was upset over his father's accident, were kinder too. But nobody could get even a half smile out of him. It was a very changed Tony who sat in class that Monday.

He was going to see young Walters in the lunch-hour. He was taking him his most precious possession – his beautiful little microscope. It had been a present to him from Aunt Grace when he was twelve and keen on using one. He knew that Tom Walters was as enthusiastic as the twins over everything to do with nature and that all of them loved to use his precious microscope when they got his permission to do so. He knew young Tom would revel in having it for his own.

Tom was sitting up in bed, looking extremely pale but quite cheerful. He had an enormous bandage on which made his head seem much bigger than usual. He looked surprised to see

Tony. 'I say, it's good of you to come!' he said. 'I've seen the twins already.'

Good of him to come! Tony stared. Hadn't anyone told Tom then that it was all his, Tony's, fault that he was here in hospital. Nobody had, apparently.

'Well, of course I came,' said Tony, rather awkwardly. 'I ought to have come before. The thing that hit you on the head was a bottle I threw out of my classroom window, Tom. Fat-headed thing to do. I'm frightfully sorry.'

'Coo!' said young Tom, his eyes opening wide. 'That's what hit me, was it? I smelled a frightful smell too. Why didn't anyone tell me?'

'I've brought you my microscope,' said Tony and put it on the bed in its neat wooden box. 'I thought you'd like it.'

'Not – not to give me?' said Tom, his white face going red.

Tony smiled and nodded. 'Yes. You have it. I'd like you to.'

'Coo!' said Tom, redder than ever. 'Mine! What'll the twins say? No, you keep it, Tony, I know you want it. You don't need to be as sorry as all that. You just lend it to me.'

'I don't want it. It's yours,' said Tony. 'Come on, let's do a jigsaw or something.'

'Coo!' said Tom, gazing at the microscope. 'I've asked and asked my father for one and he

202

always says they're too expensive. What'll he say when I show him this? Coo!'

'Anyone would think you were a dove, the way you keep cooing!' said Tony and Tom laughed his infectious chuckle.

'You're good at making people laugh, aren't you?' he said to Tony. 'Bother, there's the nurse coming to say you're to go. Do come and see me again if it's not too much of a bore. And thanks most awfully.'

Tony went out, feeling a little better. It had been hard to part with his beautiful little microscope, but he had got to get right with himself somehow. He felt better for giving it away. He could hear young Tom saying 'Coo' and he felt almost like smiling. Then the black cloud closed down on him again as he thought of the disgrace he was in. Nobody knew as yet, but they soon would!

Pam, Lizzie and Delia went off to school that day too. It was good to be back in the world of school again after the upheavals of the weekend. Lizzie especially was glad. She loved school, the companionship there, the laughter and fun, the hard work and the games. It didn't matter that she wasn't good at them, she loved them all the same.

At Break there was great excitement, and a piece of news buzzed from one classroom to another as the girls poured out. 'Exam results are out – and the scholarship results! They're on the notice-board!'

Pam felt a little surge of excitement. It would be good to see her name there, at the top, good to have everyone's congratulations, and to forget, for a while, the disgust she had felt for herself all the weekend. Lizzie caught hold of her arm.

'Come on, Pam. Let's go and see. Hope our school has got some good results!'

They rushed to the notice-board, which was already surrounded by an excited crowd of girls.

Pam glanced at the scholarship results. All the names of the entrants were there in their correct order, with their marks, and the names of the different schools that the girls came from. Only five had entered from Pam's school.

Pam's name was not at the top. It was not even second or third or fourth! In the utmost horror the girl ran her eyes down the list. Her name must be there! She had gone in for the scholarship, hadn't she?

It was there . . . fifth from the bottom! And Angela, Angela who always forgot her lines for the play, was third on the list! She was far higher than Pam.

Pam turned away, sick at heart. Now she hadn't won the scholarship, now everyone would pity her, because the whole school had been so certain that it was in her pocket! What a good thing she had been entered to go to college anyhow, whether she won the scholarship or not!

Then she had a cold feeling round her heart, as if a stony hand was squeezing it. Would she be able to go now that Daddy was ill and not likely to be able to work for some time? He would have to pay the fees instead of her winning a grant for them. She wouldn't be able to go to college!

The disappointment was too much for her.

She went blindly out into the playground and found a lonely corner. Why were all these awful things happening to her? She didn't deserve them. Now all her future plans were in ruins. She hadn't anything to look forward to at all. Everything was simply hateful and terribly, terribly unfair.

Lizzie came to find her, but Pam pushed her away. 'Don't say anything,' she said fiercely. 'I won't have anyone crowing over me!'

'Oh, Pam, as if I would,' said Lizzie, hurt. 'I only came to say how sorry I was, you poor old thing. You worked too hard at the play.'

'That play!' burst out Pam. 'It caused Daddy's accident because I wouldn't ask him to come to it and it's prevented me from winning the scholarship. Why did I ever take part in it?'

She would not be comforted by Lizzie, so the girl went away. Bad luck seemed to be coming from all quarters. Lizzie was sure Tony was in trouble. He was so unlike himself, and yet she couldn't get a word out of him. And now here was Pam getting all difficult again. Really, the Farrell family didn't hang together at all!

That evening Michael Best came over to see the twins and the rest of the family. They were all glad to see him, for, although Tony called him a prig, he secretly admired the tall, straightforward boy very much.

'I say, I'm most frightfully sorry to hear about your father,' said Michael. 'What a blow for you all!'

They talked together for a time. Michael was puzzled by Tony and Pam. They wouldn't look him in the eyes, and it seemed to him as if both were hiding some kind of secret. As if they were ashamed of something, thought Michael. It's more than grief for their father – something's worrying each of them. Tony's lost all his merriness and smiles and Pam's lost all her looks. What's the matter with them?

The twins went out into the garden with Michael. 'We want to talk to you,' said David. 'It's most important.'

They went out and sat down on a bench outside. Tony went up to his room. The twins' clear voices floated up to him and he heard Michael's replies too.

'Michael, perhaps you haven't heard about Daddy's hand,' began David. 'It's hurt so much that they don't think he'll be able to use it again for surgery, not for ages, anyhow. So that means he can't earn money, doesn't it – at doctoring, I mean?'

'I'm afraid it does,' said Michael. 'What hard luck on him.'

'Well, we can't go to that boarding-school, that's for certain,' said Delia. 'We've quite made up our minds about that. And I suppose Mr Frost will have to go too, won't he? He gets a lot of money a week, you know. We shan't be able to afford him now.'

'So we thought we could take over the garden and the hens and the fruit and everything,' said David, earnestly. 'Mr Frost says we're as good as any gardener. We could do everything, just the same as he does. And that would be a good way of saving money, wouldn't it, Michael, if we didn't have to pay Mr Frost his wages every week? If we can save on his wages by doing the work ourselves, it would be as good as earning the same amount of money, wouldn't it?'

'It would,' said Michael. 'I think you're a couple of bricks! And I tell you what, you're going to have crowds of plums, greengages, apples and pears this year. I'll help you to pick them, and we'll sell them and save up a lot more money that way!'

'Oh yes!' said the twins.

'You'll have to work very hard,' said Michael, looking round the big garden. 'There's a frightful lot to do here. I'll help in the hols but I'm off to school again in September. What about Tony? Couldn't he help?'

'Tony? Why, he never does anything except fool about,' said Delia, in her clear voice. 'He'd laugh at us if we asked him. Anyway he'd forget everything. He's no use at anything really, if it means hard work.'

Tony heard all this. He felt angry, then he frowned. He knew it was true. He had never been any use. When he had deigned to work in the garden he had left the tools out or broken the barrow or done something equally annoying. He was not a boy to be trusted and even young Delia and David knew it.

'Well, I should ask Tony, anyway,' said Michael. 'Just because he hasn't helped so far isn't to say he won't help now. I bet he'd do anything to help his father, really. Give him a chance!'

'Michael, there's something else we want to ask you,' said David. 'It's about Daddy. Do you think you could ask your father to say an extra special prayer for Daddy's hand each night, to make it better enough for him to use it again?'

'Why don't you ask God yourself?' said Michael, in surprise.

'Oh, we do, each night,' said Delia. 'But you see, your father's a rector so God would probably listen to an important man like him more than He would to us.'

'You are just as important in God's eyes as any king or priest,' said Michael. 'It isn't how important we are that matters, it's how much we love other people. The ones who are nearest to God's ear, I always think, are those who love others unselfishly with all their heart. Of course I'll ask my father, he'll be very glad to do anything for you.'

'I wish prayers came true oftener,' said Delia. 'I shall pray and pray with all my heart that Daddy's hand will be made better, but I don't expect it will.'

'Pray to God, sailor – but row for the shore!' quoted Michael. 'You know what that saying means. When you or your family are in trouble, pray to God for help but do your bit too, and

210

row hard for the shore. You go on praying to God for your father, but do all you can your-selves to help him and your mother, by working hard in the garden, picking fruit and selling it – if your father knows you're doing all that it will certainly help him to get better!'

'Pray to God, sailor – but row for the shore!' repeated Delia. 'I like that. Michael, I think you're the most sensible person I know. Aunt Grace is sensible too. You've helped us a lot, Mike, so thanks awfully.'

21

Tony 'Rows for the Shore'

Tony leaned out of his window. He had heard every word. Now he wondered if he ought to have listened. Michael was a brick, and certainly he was sensible. Tony wished he was his friend. You could go to people like Michael and tell them things you were ashamed of, and they would never laugh at you or be scornful – they would help you.

The twins went to fetch their spades. Michael made his way to the gate to go home. On an impulse Tony called to him. 'Michael! Wait for me. I'll walk home with you.'

Rather surprised, Michael waited. Tony came hurrying out. The two boys went down the lane and struck across the fields to the Rectory.

'I say, Michael,' said Tony, and stopped. It was difficult to know how to begin – what to say and what to keep back. Well, he wouldn't keep back anything! He took the plunge and raced on breathlessly.

'Michael, an awful thing's happened to me – the head's expelling me. I can't go back to school next term.'

Michael looked at him in amazement and horror. 'Tony! Do you mean it? Whatever have you done? Do your parents know?'

'No, they don't. Not yet. The head promised not to write because of Dad's accident,' said Tony. 'I've got to tell them myself. I feel such a worm.'

'But Tony – what have you done?' asked Michael again.

Tony told him everything. He told him of all the years he had wasted, the way he had fooled about, the bad time he had given Blinky – he spared himself nothing. It was the first time he had ever confessed so much to anyone.

'And now I'm expelled – just as Mum gets this awful blow,' he ended bitterly. 'I'm useless. What can I do? I can't even earn anything at my age, with my bad report too!'

It was beyond the fifteen-year-old Michael to give Tony really good advice. He saw that things were really serious. It wasn't only Tony's past that came into it – it was his future. He had brains, there wasn't a doubt of it, but there would be no brilliant career for him now. What could be done?

'Say something!' said Tony, impatiently. 'I've never told anyone so much before. Can't you give me some kind of advice? I'm worrying my heart out!'

'Tony, you come in and see my father,' said Michael. 'It wants a grown-up to see to this. Honestly it does. Dad will know what to do. He'll help you all right.'

'He's not to go running to Mum or Aunt Grace before I'm ready to tell them,' said Tony.

'Of course he wouldn't,' said Michael, indignantly. 'And don't you take that tone, either, you're in a frightful fix and Dad will try to show you the way out – but he'll be the one to say what's to be done, not you!'

'I don't know if I want to tell your father,' said Tony, when they arrived at the Rectory. Then he smiled a crooked smile at Michael. 'Still, what was that saying you quoted to the twins? "Pray to God, sailor – but row for the shore!" Well, I've got to row for the shore all right. Here goes!'

They went in. The Rector was in his study, reading. Michael took Tony in.

'Dad,' he said, 'Tony's in a spot of trouble. He wants to tell you about it. I know you'll help.'

Michael went out and shut the door. How many, many people had gone to his father in their troubles, and had been helped! The Rector could be stern and solemn, he could be gentle and kind, he saw through everyone, right into their secret hearts, and was as much loved and

respected as Mr Farrell, healer of bodies. Now here he was, faced with a frightened, miserable and foolish boy, son of one of the men he loved most.

He listened in silence. Yes, this boy was indeed in need of help – the Rector's help and God's help too. He was like one of the lost sheep, and did not know which way to go.

Tony was with the Rector for nearly two hours. What happened in that study he never told anyone. When he came out, red-eyed, he looked a different boy. He was at peace with himself once more. He knew what to do, and what was more, he had the strength to do it. He went to find Michael.

'Michael, it's all right,' he said. 'I've found out what to do. Your father is fine, really fine. Mike, be my friend as well as the twins' and help me, will you?'

'Like a shot,' said Michael. 'Won't the twins be surprised!'

'Your father suggests I should go to Farmer Grant for the holidays and work on the land for him,' said Tony. 'I'm big and strong for my age and he wants workers for the harvest. I can earn money too, that way. He says not to look too far ahead, but just to do that straightaway at the end of the week, and discuss plans for next autumn with my own father when he's well enough. He says he'll talk to him, too, see if they can find out the best thing to do. The whole worry's gone from my shoulders now.'

'Farmer Grant's a good fellow,' said Michael. 'He'll work you hard, Tony, but farm-work is always hard work. And you'll have a bit of money to take home too. Jolly good idea. I suppose you won't have time to help me with the Scouts, will you? I could do with some help.'

'I'll help you in anything!' said Tony, feeling that he could even help with the cooking at home, his heart felt so much lighter! 'Anything, Mike! You've only got to ask me.'

Tony went home, almost whistling again. He felt cleaner somehow. He had told everything and kept back nothing, not even the fact that he had been too cowardly to ask how Tom was at the hospital. He knew what to do, and he was going to do it. And wouldn't he work hard with Farmer Grant! No fooling about there.

The week went by and both schools broke up. The news continued good from the hospital where Mr Farrell was. Tony went to see Tom Walters every day and took him books and fruit. The twins went to see him too. In fact, as Tom said, he was jolly glad he'd had the accident – he'd missed an exam or two, and was getting more fussing and presents than he'd ever had in his life!

'I told Dad you'd given me your microscope, Tony,' he said. 'He didn't say a word. But he was jolly surprised.'

Pam had asked Lizzie to tell Aunt Grace about her failure to win the scholarship, and to tell her mother too. She said she simply couldn't. So Lizzie broke the news.

'I'm not surprised,' was all that Aunt Grace said. But Mrs Farrell was distressed and worried.

'Hasn't won it – Pam hasn't won the scholarship?' she kept saying. 'But then we'll have to pay the fees – and we can't now. Oh dear, will troubles never end? What in the world shall we do with Pam? She'll simply hate being at home, and she won't like taking a poorly-paid job.'

Then Tony announced that he was going to work with Farmer Grant on the next Monday. Everyone gasped.

'Oh no, dear, there's no need to do that,' said Mrs Farrell. 'It would be far too hard for you.'

'Hard for him with his strong body and brawny arms?' said Aunt Grace. 'Don't be silly, Lucy. Do him all the good in the world, and I must say I'm very pleasantly surprised, and he goes up in my estimation for having character enough to find a job himself!'

'It was the Rector's idea,' said Tony. 'He went to see Farmer Grant for me and spoke for me. I'm strong enough, Mum, and I want to bring in a bit of money for you too.'

'Dear boy!' said his mother. 'How pleased your father will be. Well, you'll be out in the open air, and I shall see you at breakfast and supper – and if Farmer Grant works you too hard, I'll speak to him.'

'Mum! Don't you dare to say anything to him at all!' said Tony, in horror. 'I'm taking a man's job, and you can't possibly go and "speak" to the farmer. I shall be so ashamed. I'm going to work very hard and enjoy it.'

'Quite right, Tony,' said Aunt Grace. 'I'll see that your mother doesn't do any "speaking" to the farmer!' Everyone laughed, even Pam. Mrs Farrell so often 'spoke' to people, when she didn't approve of something they did, and the family teased her about it.

Pam had been very quiet since she had heard the scholarship results. It had been a great shock to her pride. She had found it difficult to hold up her head and be brave about it, the last few days at school.

The headmistress had said a few words to her when she left. 'Pam, I am very distressed about your losing the scholarship,' she said. 'Especially now, when your family would have been glad of it. I blame myself very, very much for letting you take the chief part in the school play. It was that that prevented you from doing well in the exam.'

'I'm not sure about that, Miss Dawes,' said Pam in a humbler voice than usual. 'I felt so certain I could win it – I don't believe I should have worked hard enough even if I hadn't done the play. If I'd known I'd never have thought of the play, but would have gone all out for the scholarship.'

'Ah, yes, if we could see into the future we might do lots of things differently,' said Miss Dawes. 'Have you thought at all what you will do, Pamela, if you don't go to college?'

'No, Miss Dawes,' said Pamela. 'You see, I don't know about Daddy yet, what he'll be able to do.'

'You may find it is your duty to stay at home and help your mother,' said Miss Dawes. 'After all, there are younger brothers and sisters, Pamela, and your mother must have some help.'

'Oh, there's Lizzie,' said Pam. 'She'll like to help.'

'But Lizzie will still be at school!' said Miss Dawes. 'Surely you would not allow your younger sister to take your place in the household and leave school before she should, Pamela? I have sometimes thought you are growing selfish, my dear, and think too much of your own future and yourself. Your family is weathering great trouble just now, you should think of them first and foremost and yourself last of all. It may possibly even be a good thing that you have not won the scholarship, because now you can take your share of the family tasks and help your mother with the younger children.'

Pamela was horrified at the thought. After all her high hopes, to be stuck at House at the Corner, seeing to those twins, and making Tony's bed and getting hot in the kitchen! She forgot that to Jean these would be lovely and natural things to do, that to Lizzie there was something very satisfactory in doing jobs for people she loved. She couldn't get used to thinking of herself as anything but a clever girl with a brilliant future.

All the same, her headmistress's words sank in, and she began to think of herself as one of a family, sharing their ups and downs, and not somebody separate, going her own way. She was quiet and thoughtful that week, though she still had black times when she reproached herself bitterly for, as she thought, being the cause of her father's accident.

But she still hoped somehow to get a splendid job. She clung to the thought that surely, with her cleverness, someone would want her to fill an excellent post. One day she would be the clever, talented, pretty Miss Farrell and everyone would envy her. Poor Lizzie, she thought, she thinks she'll look better without her glasses, but she won't! It's hard luck on her – but I shall always be the pretty, popular Miss Farrell, whilst Lizzie sticks in a corner!

Pam was slow at learning her lessons – but it is hard to change yourself when you are as old as eighteen!

22

A Family Council

It was clear that the Farrell family would soon have to hold a council to decide what was going to be done.

'We'd better have a family meeting, a real family council, with everyone there, even the twins,' said Aunt Grace. 'Better to do that than to decide things by ourselves, Lucy. Let the children take their part, and shoulder their bit of responsibility. We have got to plan something now. It's plain that John's work can't be taken up for at least a year or two, he'll have to have all kinds of treatment for that hand of his if he's ever going to use it again.'

'Yes, I suppose we must have a family council, though why we should have those babies taking part in it, I can't think,' said Mrs Farrell. 'What use would the twins be in a meeting like that? It would only worry them.'

'For goodness' sake, Lucy, stop calling them babies!' said Aunt Grace, clicking her knitting-needles loudly, as she always did when she felt exasperated. 'They're worth half a dozen Pams and Tonies! There now – I shouldn't have said that – but really you are most aggravating at times!'

Mrs Farrell looked hurt. She thought the world of her eldest daughter and son. 'Well, we'll have them all in the council,' she said. 'Better get them round us tonight.'

So that night, after supper, all the Farrells, except Mr Farrell, gathered round the big

dining-room table to discuss their future plans. The twins were there too, of course, solemn and grave, more grown-up even than Pam in their determination to do their share!

Mrs Farrell began. 'Children, you know why I want to talk to you. You know that Daddy's accident will make it very difficult to keep things going for a while – till we see what power and skill come back to his poor right hand – so Aunt Grace and I thought it would be a good thing for us all to discuss the future year or two together.'

She paused and looked round at the five earnest faces of her children. 'We can't give up our house and garden because if Daddy can work again he will need it and the consulting room. So somehow we must keep that going. But how, I don't know!'

Aunt Grace laid down her ever-busy needles. 'I have a suggestion to make, first of all,' she said. 'This is a big house and a very pleasant one. Couldn't you take in two or three paying guests – people who would be very glad to live here and have good, well-cooked food, pleasant surroundings, and a happy home? Whilst your father is not using his consulting room it could be made into a private sitting-room. Guests would pay well for a good home like this – the money would be a very great help.'

225

Pam didn't like the idea, but said nothing. Lizzie spoke up at once. 'Yes, of course we could do that! Of course we could, Aunt Grace. I could leave school and help every day – I could do all the cooking, I'm sure!'

'But, my dear, you would hate to leave school,' said Aunt Grace. 'You should have two more years there.'

'Well, I do love school, though I'm not awfully good at lessons,' said Lizzie. 'But I like my family better! If that would be a help I'd do it. Mummy, you could really trust me to do all the cooking! Jean would give me lessons, I know, and I'm quite good already.'

'It's sweet of you, Lizzie,' said Mrs Farrell. 'And after all, you're not very good at school subjects and you couldn't earn money at anything . . .'

Lizzie went red. She looked at her great-aunt, who nodded her head vigorously. Yes – the time had certainly come to tell the family about Lizzie's writing!

'Mummy, I've got something to tell you,' said Lizzie, her face flaming still redder. 'I've had a secret for some while now. I'm – I'm earning quite a lot of money!'

The Farrells gaped at Lizzie. They couldn't believe their ears. 'Whatever do you mean, Lizzie?' demanded Pam.

'You earning a lot of money!' said Mrs Farrell. 'How, Lizzie?'

Lizzie explained. 'Well, you see, you know I've always loved writing and I wrote some stories, and I used Daddy's typewriter, he said I could, and typed them. And I sent them to *Rivers-End Weekly* – and, oh Mummy, they asked me to write one every week – children's stories you know – and now they send me a cheque for five pounds every Thursday!'

Everyone gasped except Aunt Grace. She was really enjoying herself. Aha! What a surprise for the Farrells to find their ugly duckling turned into a swan!

Then Delia gave a squeal and flung herself on Lizzie. 'Lizzie, oh Lizzie – are they the stories that David and I have been reading in the paper each week? Are they? Tell us they are. We love them. They're wizard – the best we've ever read in that paper!'

Lizzie glowed. 'Yes, those are the stories,' she said. 'Mummy, you read the first one but you said it was silly, so I didn't tell you any more about my secret.'

'I said it was silly?' repeated Mrs Farrell, disbelievingly. 'I couldn't have! I don't remember reading the Children's Corner in the paper at all. I remember you telling me to read a story some time ago, and I read it, but it was a tale

227

for grown-ups called "Sheila's Folly" which I thought extremely stupid. What was your tale called?'

'"The Thirteen Cats",' said Lizzie. 'Oh, Mummy, you read the wrong story! If only I'd known! I was so disappointed and hurt that you called my story silly.'

'As if I would!' said Mrs Farrell, and gave Lizzie a hug. 'Well, really, Lizzie, to think you can write and have stories printed and be paid for them! I never knew that writers were paid for little stories like that.'

'Oh, Lucy, don't be so foolish,' said Aunt Grace. 'Why shouldn't they be? Lizzie and I were delighted when we saw the first one in print.'

'What – were you in the secret too?' said Mrs Farrell, a little hurt. 'And you never told me! Well, I think you might!'

'I'm not surprised that Lizzie didn't tell anyone,' said Tony. 'I was a beast about the first one when it came back, wasn't I, Liz? I remember now. And if you thought Mum said your story was silly, I don't wonder you kept your secret to yourself. But my word – five pounds a week! I bet they wouldn't pay that if they knew how old you were!'

'Do you use your own name for writing your stories?' demanded Mrs Farrell, feeling suddenly very proud of Lizzie. 'Lizzie's not a very good name for a writer.'

'No, I use my proper name, Elizabeth,' said Lizzie. 'Elizabeth Farrell – doesn't it sound nice, Mummy?'

'Yes, it certainly does,' said Mrs Farrell. 'Elizabeth Farrell, well, well, well, what a surprise! I really do think we'd better call you Elizabeth now, Lizzie.'

'Oh, please do!' cried Lizzie. 'I do so hate being called Lizzie or Liz. I feel much more like an Elizabeth than a Lizzie!'

'Well, we'll call you what you like,' said Tony. 'You deserve it, Lizzie – I mean Elizabeth. My word, this really will be a wonderful bit of news for Dad!'

'Oh yes!' said the twins. Pam said nothing. The news she had for her father was of failure, not of success. She glanced at the glowing Lizzie. Why, Lizzie must be frightfully clever to write like that. She felt a little stab of jealousy and then stifled it. No, Lizzie was good and kind and she must be glad she was successful too. She had offered to leave school and do the cooking. She was glad Lizzie was clever enough to have stories printed.

'Congratulations, Lizzie – Elizabeth, I mean,' said Pam, and squeezed her sister's arm. 'You're marvellous!'

Praise from the haughty, brilliant Pam was very rare and very sweet to Lizzie. She smiled. Then she turned to her mother.

'Mummy, I want to use my money in a special way,' she said. 'I want to pay for the twins to go to boarding-school. I know it won't nearly pay all the fees, but it would help enough to let them go, wouldn't it? They're such good little things, and they do work so hard in the garden. They deserve to have what they so much want – to go to school together!'

But before Mrs Farrell could answer, the twins spoke up for themselves.

'Thanks, Lizzie. You're wizard!' said David. 'But we're not going. We've quite made up our minds.'

'We've decided it all,' said Delia, in her clear, determined little voice. The others stared at them.

'And what exactly have you decided?' asked Aunt Grace, amused.

'Well,' said David. 'We won't be able to keep Mr Frost on now – at least not all the week, anyhow. So Delia and I are going to do the garden, grow all the vegetables, look after the hens – and we thought we'd take over Mr Frost's bees, Mum, too, if you don't mind.'

'We've been reading about them in our book,' put in Delia.

'And we're going to pick all the fruit, give Lizzie what she wants for bottling and jamming, and sell the rest,' said David. 'Michael's going to help us. He says he knows heaps of people who will buy it. He's having a special box made for the back of his bicycle so that he can take the fruit about for us.'

Mrs Farrell stared at him. This wasn't a 'baby' speaking. This was a responsible, clever and determined young man! She opened and shut her mouth, trying to think of something to say. What with Lizzie bursting this bombshell on her – and now the twins announcing what they had planned to do – why, she didn't know her children at all!

'Mummy, you don't mind, do you?' said

Delia, wondering why her mother said nothing. 'You see, if we take over the garden – and we can, quite easily, winter and summer – we can save you Mr Frost's wages – and we can give you a lot of money from the fruit if you'll let us and Michael sell it. Just fancy, one of the greengage trees has about fifteen pounds' worth of fruit on this year, Mike says.'

There was a silence. Pam gaped in amazement at the self-possessed pair of twins, so earnest in their resolve to help. Aunt Grace swallowed a lump in her throat. What a pair they were! Ready to give up their cherished plan of going to Whyteleafe together without a grumble or a murmur – ready to slave hard at school and then in the garden, every week. Bless them! thought Aunt Grace, and blew her nose hard.

'So thank you very, very much, Lizzie, for your offer to spend your money on us,' said David, beaming at his sister. 'But we couldn't take it now. No one else can do the garden but us. We wondered if Tony could give a hand with the digging sometimes. That clay patch at the bottom is a bit heavy.'

Now it was Tony's turn to speak. How glad he was that he could really offer help too! 'Of course I'll dig for you, twins,' he said. 'Mum, you know I'm going to Farmer Grant's on Monday, don't you? I shall give you every penny I earn, so that will be a bit of help too, I hope.'

'My dear boy!' said Mrs Farrell. 'You're all so good and sweet – but Tony dear, you can only work two months on the farm, as long as the holidays last. You must go back to school then, you know. Your father and I will insist on that. You can't spoil your future by leaving school. Only two months on the farm, dear!'

Tony was silent. His mother didn't know that he couldn't go back to school because he had been expelled. Mrs Farrell looked at him.

'Tony! Don't sit dumb like that! You must promise me to go back to school after the holidays. I'm not going to let your ideas about farmwork spoil you for school. Now, promise me, Tony, or I won't let you go to the farm on Monday. Give me your solemn promise!'

23

Tony breaks his News

Tony was in despair. He couldn't promise his mother! He wouldn't be allowed to go back, but she didn't know why. He stared at her, wondering what to say. He must go to work on the farm, he must. He would get back a little of his self-respect then and feel happier.

'Tony!' said Aunt Grace, sharply, thinking that the boy was being silly and obstinate. 'Answer your mother.'

Tony gave a gulp. He was concerned. Things would have to be told now – in front of everyone, too! Well, they would have to know sometime.

'Mum, I can't go back to school next term,' he said, in a low voice. 'I've been expelled.'

He looked at the floor, crimson to the tips of his ears. Pam gave a gasp of horror. Lizzie gazed disbelievingly at him. The twins looked at one another.

'Was it because that bottle of yours hit Tom on the head?' said David. 'Well, it's a shame! That was an accident. I suppose you owned up after all?'

'It wasn't only because of that,' said Tony, not daring to look at his mother. 'It was because I'd fooled about so much and the head said – he said I was a bad influence on the boys, Mum. He said awful things. I can't tell you. He promised not to write to you just now or you would have known. Mum, I'm so terribly sorry. Now you see why I can't promise not to go back to school next term.'

Mrs Farrell stared at Tony. Tears rolled down her cheeks but she did not wipe them away. 'Tony,' she whispered, 'I was so proud of you. I was so proud of you. How could you do such a thing to me?'

'Mum, don't!' said poor Tony. 'I'll make it up to you some day, I swear I will. I've told the Rector all about it and he got me the job. He's going to talk to Dad. Mum, don't look like that, I can't bear it!'

Mrs Farrell got up, put out her hands almost as if she was blind, and stumbled out of the room. The council was over as far as she was concerned. Lizzie got up to follow her, but Aunt Grace pulled her back.

'No,' she said. 'Let her think this out for herself. It's a terrible shock – it is to us all, of course. Poor Tony has had a terrible lesson. I wondered what was the matter. Well, Tony you've made a fool of yourself, and the only thing left to do

is to patch things up, and do the best you can. It's a pity this happened just now.'

Tony swallowed hard before he could speak. It had been terrible for him to see his mother's grief. That was the worst of doing wrong – its effects fell on other people too, people you loved. He set his teeth together and vowed never to fail again. He'd show his family he could do well somehow!

'We'd better go on with our council,' said Aunt Grace, her sound common sense making everyone feel a little better. 'We seem to be deciding a few things, anyway. It's plain that Tony can't go back to his school. He'd better take up this farm-work for the present, anyway. The twins will stay at their present schools and take over the garden, bless them. And we will take in two paying guests, and look after them well. I shall be one guest – and I will bring my friend, Mrs Young, for the other. I know she would like to come.'

'Oh, Aunt Grace, we couldn't possibly let you pay to live here!' said Lizzie at once. 'You're such a help!'

'What's Pam going to do?' said Delia. 'We haven't decided anything about Pam yet.'

Lizzie leaned forward, her eyes shining behind her glasses. 'Well, if the twins won't go to boarding-school, I can use the money for Pam. She will be able to go to college after all. Pam, you can go! I can earn the money for you, easily, and I can leave school and see to everything for Mummy.'

Pam's heart leaped. Go to college after all! Then she looked at generous, warm-hearted Lizzie, who was giving up her money and her school-life for her. She looked at the twins who had so cheerfully changed their plans and taken on hard work – at Tony, trying to make amends and going to earn money on the farm. Something happened to her hard little heart. It seemed to break in half, then it swelled up and hurt her. It grew warm and loving.

She heard herself speaking quickly. 'No, Lizzie, no! You shan't spend a penny on me, not a penny! And you shan't leave school. I won't have it! I am going to be the one to come home and do the work. I can't cook but I'll soon learn. I'll learn all the things Jean says I ought to know, the real things, the things that matter in every home, and I'll do them well. I won't go to college, so it's no good saying a word more!'

She paused, out of breath. Aunt Grace, absolutely amazed, hadn't a word to say. She had even dropped her knitting-needles. Tony suddenly thumped on the table. The twins, infected by the general amazement and delight at Pam's sudden change of heart, began to clap as if they were at a concert!

'Good old Pam!' squealed Delia. 'I never thought you could do a thing like that!'

'I didn't think I could myself,' said Pam, surprised at what she had been saying. 'But I mean it. We're one family and I belong to it as much as you do, and I'm going to pull together with you. You see if I don't. I've been an idiot too – failed in my scholarship, serves me right – and – yes – I've been an awful beast, haven't I, Aunt Grace?'

'You certainly have,' said Aunt Grace, with much feeling. 'I've wanted to slap you plenty of times. But it's never too late to mend.'

'Oh, Pam, I don't want you to come home and not go to college,' began Lizzie. But Aunt Grace stopped her.

'Now, we've had plenty of generosity from you tonight, Elizabeth,' she said, 'you must let others show generosity too, and what is more, accept it. Pam will have two months to learn things from you and Jean before you go back to school, and she'll never regret it. She and Tony are taking the right way to make amends – no more wailing and sulking but good hard work and facing up to things. I tell you, even if we do wrong, we can make some good come out of it if we really want to. Your father will be upset, Tony, to hear of your expulsion, but glad to know you have character enough to make amends and get a job. He will be sad to know you have failed in the scholarship, Pam, but delighted to see you taking your part in the home. Out of wrong and stupidity you will force something worthwhile.'

Even the twins understood this and approved. There was something brave and courageous about it. 'Am I knocked down? Well, I'll get up!' That was the idea behind Aunt Grace's little lecture, and it was a good one.

'You ought to preach in the Rector's pulpit, Aunt Grace,' said David, earnestly. 'You'd be awfully good. I'm sure everyone would listen to you.'

They all laughed, picturing Aunt Grace standing up in the pulpit, settling her glasses firmly on her nose.

'I know what you'd say first of all,' said Delia, giggling. 'You'd say, "Now where's my hanky?"'

'Don't be cheeky,' said Aunt Grace, delighted to see smiles on everyone's faces. 'Well, my dears, that's everything settled then – and I and Mrs Young come as paying guests and I'll arrange payment with your mother – but mind, Pam, I shall want really good cooking and waiting on, and so will Mrs Young. We shall make you very busy indeed!'

'I'll do my best,' said Pam. 'I know Jean will give me plenty of tips.'

'And Lizzie will go back to school,' went on Aunt Grace. 'And Tony will do farm-work – at least till his father arranges what is to be done with him – and the twins go back to school too, and we give Mr Frost notice so that they can take over the garden. Well, we've settled everything very satisfactorily, I think!'

She went to find Mrs Farrell, who had quite given way. Her bright boy, Tony! How could

this have happened to him? And Pam had failed in her scholarship too. Why were so many dreadful things happening to her all at once?

'Listen, Lucy,' said Aunt Grace, sitting on the bed and taking her hand. 'Things like this happen in every family, and we have to make the best of them. You spoilt both Pam and Tony, gave them all they wanted, let them grow up selfish and headstrong. You thought it was enough that Pam was brilliant and pretty, and that Tony was clever and amusing. It wasn't, and they've each failed dismally. But they are both genuinely sorry and want to make amends. It's not going to help them if you give way like this and cry and reproach them, is it?'

'You don't understand, Aunt Grace,' said Mrs Farrell, pulling her hand away.

'Rubbish!' said Aunt Grace. 'Of course I do. The onlooker sees most of the game, you know! It's partly your fault, Lucy, that Pam and Tony were failures; now you too must make amends for that and help them.'

'You're very hard, Aunt Grace,' said Mrs Farrell, dabbing her eyes, and sitting up.

'My dear, I'm not really,' said Aunt Grace, in a gentler tone. 'Lucy, you want more backbone – you've got your wishbone where your backbone ought to be!'

Mrs Farrell couldn't help smiling. 'You say such silly things, Aunt Grace!' she said. 'What happened after I went?'

Aunt Grace told her. Mrs Farrell hardly knew what to say when she heard that Pam had refused Lizzie's offer and meant to come home and work so that Lizzie could finish her schooling.

'It's the very best thing she could do,' said Aunt Grace. 'Lucy, you've loved being married and having a home of your own to run, being the centre of it, giving the children dinners you've planned and often cooked, seeing them eat your lovely marrow jam, welcoming John home, caring for your home and family with pride and love, haven't you?'

'Of course,' said Mrs Farrell.

'Well, you give Pam a chance of learning how to run a home for a bit, let her feel the joy of having the family turning to her, let her mend and sew, cook and clean,' said Aunt Grace. 'She'll be a woman then, and all the better for knowing what every woman ought to know, no matter what job she takes afterwards. And when she comes to marry she'll make a good wife and mother. You leave things to her, Lucy, and don't spoil her any more!'

'I wonder what poor John will say when he hears about Tony and Pam,' said Mrs Farrell, suddenly thinking of her husband.

'He's not going to hear a word about it till he's fit to hear it,' said Aunt Grace. 'Not a word, Lucy. We won't cross our bridges till we come to them. We'll just let things go on as we've planned now. Do wash your face and come down. Really, you seem as much of a child as the others!'

The whole family were much happier when they went to bed that night. The twins were full of plans for the garden, and Pam had to rap on the wall to make them stop calling out to one another at half past ten! Lizzie couldn't help feeling pleased that she wouldn't have to leave school after all. Tony was glad that the family knew the worst about him. Now he could get on with his farm-work happily.

As for Pam, she felt a different person. She was sharing the troubles and burdens of the family. She was really one of them. It wasn't as hard as she had thought to give up all her plans and think of the plans of others instead. But it would be hard to buckle to and run the house! Still, she'd do it. She had brains and determination and she could do it!

She set the kitchen alarm clock for half past six. Nothing like beginning at once! She'd be down long before Lizzie and get things going. She failed in one thing – but she'd make a success of *this* job, no matter how hard it was.

24

The Holidays go By

The holidays slipped away. The twins took on the garden and worked there all day long. Old Frost still came once a week to direct things and keep them going. He was full of loud praise for 'they two young-uns' and his wife listened patiently each Friday evening to long tales of their good work.

'They've tied up all the celery proper-like,' related Frost. 'And they've staked up the Indian corn – my, it's that high this year! And they've got more eggs out of them hens than ever. Proper little workmen they are. The hoeing and weeding they do fair gets me.'

Tony went to work on the farm. At first he found that he could hardly get up in the mornings. He was stiff and tired. But he kept on, and soon lost his stiffness and rejoiced in his strong muscles and sturdy body, as he harvested the corn and helped the farmer with his cattle.

He saw Michael every day, for the boy was also helping the farmer, though only for half a day, as he had many other things to do. Tony kept his word and helped him with the Scouts and enjoyed it. The two boys ran Mrs Best's old ladies' outing for her too, and the women were loud in their praise of 'they two young men' who fetched and carried and waited on them so willingly. The Rector was pleased with his old friend's son and watched Tony's progress with the greatest interest – and with pride too, for he saw that the boy was determined to put every ounce of energy and drive into his work that he could.

Farmer Grant spoke to the Rector after a week or two. 'That's a fine lad you've sent me,' he said. 'He's only fourteen, but I can trust him more than many a man. Got a good memory and uses it. Never forgets a job and does it as well as I could. He's a great help to me.'

'Good,' said the Rector. 'Keep him at it, Mr Grant. Don't let him slack for a minute.'

Lizzie was helping Pam in the house, and Jean came in often to help as well. Mrs Farrell was only allowed to do things like the flowers, or write letters, when she was not at the hospital. Aunt Grace was not allowed to do anything either, now she was paying for her board and lodging. She didn't altogether like this, but when she saw how capably the girls were running the house, she gave way, and felt pleased.

Her friend, Mrs Young, had arrived and was installed in Pam's bedroom, which she had given up. Pam herself had gone into Greta's old room. It was a dear little room under the eaves, with a wonderful view of the surrounding country. But Pam hadn't much time now for admiring views, or dreaming wonderful dreams. Her thoughts were full of dinners and shopping, fruit-bottling and jam-making. The twins brought in plenty of fruit and it had to be bottled at the right moment, when it was ripe enough, but not too ripe.

The twins also sold the surplus fruit, with Michael's help. They brought a lot of money in to their mother in this way. She didn't altogether like it, for she had been used to giving away so much.

'Well, Mum, we give away plenty, as well as selling it,' said David. 'We always give Mr Frost some on Fridays for Mrs Frost. And we give Michael plenty for the old ladies and the people who can't afford it. You can trust us to be generous as well as business-like.'

'I just can't get used to you being so grown-up!' said their mother, looking at the pile of money they had just brought her. She had Tony's wages each week too. He gave her every penny. She thought of him with pride once more. His hard outdoor work had given him a deep tan, he had grown taller and broader, and he seemed so dependable now. His father was delighted with his looks when Tony went to see him at the hospital.

Tony had remained friends with little Tom, who came often to help the twins in the garden. Soon Tom followed him like a little dog, and even asked his father if he couldn't go and do farm-work like Tony!

Mr Walters couldn't help being interested in the boy he had seen that terrible afternoon, the boy he had wanted to cane. He had seemed such a young scamp, by all reports an empty-headed, irresponsible young rascal and yet here he was working like a man, and Farmer Grant was always praising him to Mr Walters whenever he saw him, as he often did.

Mr Walters did not give Tony away to the farmer; he did not tell him of the boy's expulsion and bad report. He was puzzled because his Tom obviously admired Tony so much and was always wanting to be with him. He knew that Tony had given Tom his precious microscope – and now here he was, in Farmer Grant's good books, and a firm friend of Michael Best, the Rector's son. Most extraordinary.

Lizzie was enjoying herself. She knew so much more about the household than Pam did, and it was nice to be able to tell Pam so many things she didn't know. Pam had always been so very good at airing her own opinions and showing off her knowledge. Now it was Lizzie's turn.

Also, Lizzie had been to the oculist and to the dentist. The wire round her teeth had gone, for her front teeth were now in place. Her glasses were gone too, for her eyes were completely better.

When she had come home, radiant without her glasses, and smiled, showing no ugly wire, her mother had stared at her. 'Why, Lizzie – you're quite pretty!' she had said, in astonishment. 'What's happened to you? No glasses, of course – but really, you're getting quite pretty!'

Lizzie had blushed and gone to look at herself. Yes, she certainly looked like Miss Elizabeth Farrell today, with her shining eyes, white, even teeth, pretty hair and rosy cheeks. She felt sure of herself, confident and happy.

The family were gradually getting used to calling her Elizabeth. Now, she thought, looking at herself half shyly in the glass, now they'll find it easier still. I don't even look like Lizzie any more!

The holidays sped by. Mrs Young proved to be rather an exacting guest, demanding all kinds of specially-cooked food and a lot of waiting on. She kept Pam very busy indeed. But not once did the girl complain, and each night her alarm clock was set for half past six as usual. Aunt Grace, watching her, felt proud of her.

Then there came a day when Lizzie had a shock. A letter came from the *Rivers-End Weekly* saying that for the present they were discontinuing their Children's Corner and would therefore not need any more stories. Their other papers were to run a new feature. They thanked Lizzie for her good work, and enclosed her the last cheque due to her.

The girl rushed to Aunt Grace, her face as long as a fiddle. She showed her the letter. 'Just when we want the money!' she said. 'Oh, Aunt Grace!'

'My dear child, there are plenty of other papers to try,' said her great-aunt. 'And you don't need money as badly as you thought. With the twins going on at the same day schools, Pam not going to college, Frost only here once a week, and Tony earning a little, we're quite all right. Now don't look so gloomy. This sort of shock comes to every writer at some time or other. It simply means you must try again somewhere else and it will all be very good experience for you!'

Mr Farrell was now very much better. He was to leave the hospital and go to see a specialist in London, staying there for a night. Then he was to come back home. How all the children looked forward to that!

Mr Farrell looked forward to it too. He had missed being at home so much. He loved his family and home, and longed for them continually. He worried about his hand, but he would know the worst very soon and he must wait in patience. He still had pain in the fingers, but not so much as he had feared. Once the hand was out of plaster he would know what he could do with it and what he couldn't do.

The great day came for him to leave the hospital. He went up to London, Mrs Farrell driving the car very slowly and carefully, for since her husband's accident she had been afraid of cars.

The children prepared for their father's homecoming the next day. He knew now about Pam's failure to win the scholarship and had been told by Aunt Grace about Tony's disgrace. He had been very silent and thoughtful, and had said hardly anything about them at all. Aunt Grace herself had said very little.

'You must remember, John,' she said, 'that what matters most is, not the failure, but the result – not the fall, but picking themselves up! Both children are doing their best now, and I think you will still be proud of them one day.'

Flowers were put into vases, ready for their father's home-coming. Delia found a dishful of late raspberries, his favourite fruit. Tony brought home a jug of cream from the farm. All his papers and journals were neatly arranged by his chair. Daddy had been away so long – how lovely to welcome him home again!

Pam refused to let anyone cook dinner for him but herself. 'I want him to see how well I can do it,' she said. 'You can do the flowers for the table, Elizabeth. That's all I shall let you do!'

The twins watched at the gate for their father and mother. They gave a hair-raising yell when they saw the familiar car. 'He's coming, he's coming!'

What a welcome for him! Five pairs of loving arms round him, hugs and kisses and howls of delight – and screeches from Sukie the parrot, 'Hip-hip-hooray! Hip-hip-hip-hip-hip-hip. . .'

Mrs Young had gone, well satisfied with her two months' stay at House at the Corner. There

was only the family left, with Aunt Grace beaming as usual behind the children. Mr Farrell
somehow got into the house, with the five children clinging like limpets.

'Welcome home, Daddy! Welcome home!'
cried Delia's clear young voice.

'We grew the vegetables for dinner!' said
David. 'We manage the garden now, Daddy.'

Aunt Grace disentangled the excited children
from their father. 'Mind his hand,' she said. 'Be

careful now! Did you see the specialist, John? Delia, don't yell in his ear like that! Come upstairs and wash, John – this hall is like a bear-garden!'

Mr Farrell was delighted with the dinner. He praised the flowers. He praised the vegetables. He praised the cooking, the dish of raspberries, the cream. He noticed everything just as he always had done.

'Daddy, can we come and sit with you after dinner and talk, like we used to do?' demanded Delia. 'We want to know such a lot – and we've got such a lot to tell you. We never seemed to have time to tell you everything when we visited you at the hospital. Can we all come and talk after dinner?'

'Of course,' said Mr Farrell. 'Oh dear, there's a very familiar noise, the phone bell ringing!'

It was the Rector, asking after his old friend, delighted to know that he had arrived back safely. 'Can I come along after dinner and bring a friend with me, who wants to say a word or two?' asked the Rector. 'Right. See you later!'

'Who's the friend?' asked David, in surprise. 'Does he mean Michael? Well, who then?'

But nobody knew and nobody really cared. Daddy was back, that was all that mattered. 'I bet we'll be allowed to go to bed late tonight,' said David to Delia. 'I feel it in the air!'

25

Happy Ending!

'Well,' said Mr Farrell after dinner, 'well, this is like old times again! All of us together. You don't know how I've missed being at home.'

'Daddy, tell us about your hand now,' begged Delia, stroking the bandages very lightly. 'What did the specialist say? Is it better?'

'As I expect you saw from your mother's face, we had very good news today,' said her father. 'My hand will be all right in time – I shall be able to use it for my work! You don't know what that means to me, children.'

'Oh Daddy, it's a miracle, surely!' cried Delia. Her father nodded at her, smiling.

'Yes – it really is a miracle!' he said. 'I was afraid it would never be any good again. I shan't be able to work for a year, then I shall begin gradually using it for operations.'

'A miracle!' said David. He looked at Delia. 'Delia, we've got a miracle!'

'What do you mean?' said their mother, amused.

'Well, we prayed and prayed that Daddy's hand would get better, really better – but we knew it would be a real miracle if it did, every-body said so,' said Delia. 'But we went on and on, and so did Michael, and the Rector did too, Daddy, because he promised us he would. We thought God would surely listen to such an important person, even if He didn't pay much attention to us. And now the miracle's hap-pened, hasn't it?'

'It's happened, thank God,' said Mr Farrell. 'I don't know what ... well, I needn't think about what would have happened now – the thing is, I shall be able to work again. We've only got a year or so to get over, and things will be the same again. It won't be too late for the twins to go to Whyteleafe then; we can manage about sending Pam to college next year too, even if she's a bit older than the other girls will be, and ...'

'Well, now, John, I have a proposal to make,' interrupted Aunt Grace. 'A large sum of money has just been paid to me for some shares I had. I was going to invest it in something else – but I think instead I'll invest it in the Farrell family!'

Everyone looked at her in surprise. What did she mean? She turned to Mr Farrell.

'I'll lend it to you, John, at the same interest as I should get if I invested it. There will be enough to send Pam to college straightaway, and the twins to Whyteleafe, and keep Lizzie at

school. I only ask one thing in return.' She paused and smiled round at the listening family.

'I'm so happy here with you all. Let me stay on – as a paying guest, of course – and live with you, and share in all your ups and downs. Oh, I know I'm an interfering, sharp-tongued old woman, always setting you all to rights, but I love each one of you, and I do long for a home of my own, here, at House at the Corner!'

'Aunt Grace, you're welcome here as long as ever you care to stay!' said Mr Farrell, patting her hand. 'You belong to the family as much as anyone!'

'Yes, you do!' cried Lizzie, and gave her great-aunt a hug. Delia followed suit.

'We couldn't possibly have done without you all this time,' said Mrs Farrell. 'As for the money – well, I don't know. John has never liked borrowing money.'

'I don't mind borrowing from Aunt Grace,' said Mr Farrell, smiling. 'I've done that before, when I was struggling to begin as a surgeon, didn't I, Aunt Grace?'

'Yes, and you paid back every single penny of it!' said Aunt Grace. 'John, I wouldn't have offered it to you at the beginning of the holidays for anything in the world because I didn't think that some of the Farrell family were worth bothering about then – but I do now.'

'What do you mean?' asked Mr Farrell, in surprise.

'Well, they've all astonished me so much these holidays,' said Aunt Grace. 'Those that I thought badly of have done well, and those that I thought well of have done better than I hoped.'

Mrs Farrell nodded in agreement. 'Yes,' she said, 'they've all been marvellous.'

'John, Pam deserves to go to college now,' said Aunt Grace. 'She has found her place in the family, she has worked hard and well, she has learned a great many of the things that all women should know. She has used those good brains of hers, and the house has run like clockwork. I shall send her to college!'

Pam went red with pleasure at this praise, which she hadn't expected at all. Her heart lifted and sang. She could go to college after all – she had earned it this time. Then her face fell.

'Yes, but Lizzie – I mean Elizabeth – can't leave school and look after things,' she said. 'And Mother can't do it all herself.'

'Wait a minute, wait a minute,' said Aunt Grace. 'You might guess I wouldn't let Elizabeth leave school. She must certainly go back, and go on with her classes. We are all proud of her and her writing, and I wouldn't dream of letting her take your place here.'

'Oh! I suppose you mean we'll get somebody to help,' said Pam, relieved. 'Oh, Aunt Grace, you really are a brick! Good gracious, I'll have to bestir myself though, college opens in five days and there are all my clothes to get!'

'You can see to those quite well in the time,' said Aunt Grace, smiling at Pam's pretty, excited face. The sulky mouth was gone. There was no ugly frown-line in the middle of her forehead. Next to her sat Lizzie, happy and smiling too. A couple of pretty young things, thought Aunt Grace. What a change in Pam's character, and Lizzie's looks.

'Now about the twins,' she said. 'I have asked Mr Frost to come back and he is delighted to. So the twins will have their wish and go to Whyteleafe after all, and they too deserve it, for if ever I saw two children work hard day and night, those two did. The garden is a picture and the kitchen garden is quite marvellous!'

'Oh, Aunt Grace, we loved doing it,' said Delia. 'We did really. And Tony helped a lot. And now that we've made up our minds we're not going to boarding-school we don't mind sticking to it a bit and not going. We'd hardly like to give up the garden now.'

'You'll like it all right when you've given it up and find yourselves at Whyteleafe!' said Aunt Grace. 'Lucy, you've got three days to see to their clothes. I hope you can do it!'

'You're taking my breath away, Aunt Grace,' said Mrs Farrell, hardly knowing if she was on her head or her heels with all these sudden proposals and decisions. 'John – what do you say to all this?'

'I think it sounds remarkably sensible,' said her husband, enjoying the family excitement. 'Wrong-doing should always be punished and usually is in some way or other, but equally, I think, goodness should be rewarded, and certainly these children have done well!'

'But, Daddy – Aunt Grace – what about poor

Tony?' said Delia, suddenly. 'You haven't said anything about him. Daddy, he's worked awfully hard too. Everybody says so. Wouldn't another school take him?'

'Well,' said Mr Farrell, 'that's the difficulty. Most decent schools nowadays are absolutely full and all they say when I apply to them for Tony, and send in his last report, which I have to do, is – we're sorry, but we have no vacancy. It is a very serious thing to be expelled, a great handicap to any career. I'm afraid it has got about that Tony has been sent off in disgrace.'

'Poor Tony – when he's tried so hard!' said Delia, indignantly. 'They might give him a chance.'

Steps were heard on the gravel outside. The Rector popped his head in at the window. 'Hello, hello!' he said. 'All at home, I see! Hello, John, delighted to see you back again. We've missed you very much. Can I bring in a friend of mine? He wants to say something rather urgently.'

'Of course,' said Mr Farrell. 'Er – is it private?'

'No,' said the Rector. 'I'll bring him in at the side-door. I see it's open.'

'Do you know who his friend is?' said Delia, in a frightened whisper. 'It's that awful Mr Walters – the man who was so angry with you, Tony.'

261

The door opened and in came the Rector and Mr Walters. Tony was embarrassed. He hadn't seen Mr Walters, except in the distance, since that terrible afternoon. He shook hands with him, blushing as he remembered all that Mr Walters had once said to him.

'Sit down,' said Mrs Farrell.

In a few minutes the reason for the unexpected visit became clear. 'You remember, John, that it was Mr Walters' boy who got hurt in that accident, when Tony threw the bottle out of the window?' said the Rector. 'Mr Walters was very angry about it – and it was he who demanded that Tony should be expelled, or he would bring a law-suit against the school. The head agreed that Tony should go. Now, Mr Walters?'

Mr Walters cleared his throat and spoke in his deep voice. 'Well, Mr Farrell,' he began, 'I was very angry, and rightly so. I would have punished young Tony severely – but you'd been so good to Tom – and I wasn't going to have that boy in the same school as mine if I could help it. I thought he was a thoroughly bad boy, and the worst influence in the school.

'But I've been changing my mind these holidays. My Tom's got very fond of your Tony, thinks no end of him, and Tony's been good to him too, gave him his microscope, you know. And – well, to cut a long story short, I know

Farmer Grant very well, and he says your Tony's done a fine job of work for him these holidays, stuck to it properly – he thinks no end of him. And the Rector spoke well of him too, and young Michael Best's his friend. Well, there can't be so much harm in the boy as I thought – maybe he's pulled himself together, or maybe I was wrong about him.'

He stopped and cleared his throat. The Farrells sat in silence, hanging on to every word. Tony could hardly breathe.

'Well, Mr Farrell, I've been to the headmaster with the Rector here and we've had a long talk

with him, and the upshot is that Tony's to go back this next term and nothing more said! You see . . .'

But the rest of his words were lost in a babel of noise! The twins cheered and banged on the table. Lizzie kept saying, 'Oh, how wonderful, how wonderful!' Sukie the parrot squawked from her corner, and Mrs Farrell murmured, 'How good of you, Mr Walters!' over and over again.

Tony's face was crimson with astonished delight. He couldn't believe his ears! He stood up and walked over to Mr Walters. 'Thank you very much, sir,' he said. 'I'll take this chance you've given me. Thanks very much, sir.'

Mr Walters put out his hand and shook Tony's hand. 'You'll be a credit to that father of yours yet!' he said. He held out his hand to Mrs Farrell too. 'Well, I won't stay, Mrs Farrell. You'll want to talk this over. But Tony's to go back the day after tomorrow and, my word, if he doesn't get a fine report, you tell me and I'll deal with him properly!'

Everyone laughed. Then the Rector and Mr Walters went out, and Pam closed the front door behind them. She flew back into the dining-room.

'Tony! What good luck! But you really do deserve it now. I say, how decent of him to go to the head. Oh, Daddy – now we're all planned for and settled!'

'So you are,' said her father and pulled her down to her old place, on the arm of his chair. She snuggled against him.

'Daddy, I still feel so awful about your accident,' she said. 'If only I'd asked you to come to the play it would never have happened. You'd have come home to lunch and not been hurt at all!'

'It was nothing to do with that,' said her father. 'I couldn't have come to the play, even if you had begged me to. I had an urgent call and had to go off to it. The accident would have happened anyhow. Don't worry your head about that.'

The last load rolled away from Pam's heart. Every night she had worried about that and she needn't have! The accident would have happened anyhow, it wasn't her unkindness that had caused it. She need not reproach herself bitterly any more.

She turned to Aunt Grace, and spoke anxiously. 'Aunt Grace, we'll all be gone to school soon, have you got somebody else to help Mother? I really can't go to college unless you have!'

Aunt Grace looked at the clock. 'You'll find somebody in the kitchen now,' she said. 'I hope

265

you'll all approve of her. Go and see, Pam.'

The others got up too, but Aunt Grace motioned them back. 'Let Pam go first,' she said. So Pam went to the kitchen, whose every corner she knew so well now. She looked round the door.

'*Greta!*' cried Pam. 'Greta, oh Greta, have you come back? Oh, we've missed you so much. I was a pig to you, but don't be angry any more. I'll never be piggy again. Greta, I've been doing all the cooking, I'm quite good at it!'

Greta turned round, beaming, and put her arms round Pam. She bore not the slightest resentment to the girl for being so rude and selfish before.

'I have heard all about it many times!' she said. 'Your Aunt Grace has told me. She knew where I was, at my friend's, and often she came to see me to tell me about you all. I was one of the family, you know. I could not get you out of my head – and ah, the poor doctor! When I heard of his accident that weekend, I rushed round here to ask to come back, but your Aunt Grace, she would not let me!'

'Wouldn't let you – but why?' cried Pam. 'You would have been such a help, Greta.'

'Your Aunt Grace, she say to me, "No, Greta, we cannot afford you now!"' said Greta and her eyes shone with indignation. 'She say that to me, to me, who would have come for nothing. But she would not let me, no. She say, "The children must do their bit, Greta, they must prove themselves. This is their chance. They have not pulled together, Greta, and this they must learn, to help one another and to work for one another. They must hold together as a family, and this is their chance!" I do not know all that she meant, but this is why I did not come till today, when she sent for me.'

Pam understood. Artful Aunt Grace! Refusing Greta's help in order to give the Farrells a chance to prove if they were worth anything or not, if they could pull together, be a united family! And they had pulled together, they were a happy and united family now, as never before. Clever Aunt Grace – kind Aunt Grace too.

'Oh, Greta, it's lovely that you're back,' said Pam. 'Greta, I'm to go to college, and the twins are to go to Whyteleafe School after all.'

'Ah no, this I do not want, for you all to go away as soon as I come back!' said Greta, her face falling. 'Why do not the twins come to speak with me? Are they shy?'

'They don't know you're here,' said Pam, and she yelled loudly. 'Twins! Come and see who's here!'

They scampered in, followed by Lizzie and Tony, all very curious. When Delia and David saw Greta they flung themselves on her with screams of delight.

'Greta, darling Greta, you've come back! Where have you been? Are you staying? Greta, nobody makes cakes like you.'

All the children gave her an uproarious welcome and the plump little Austrian beamed with delight. This was her family, she had taken them to her heart and she would not let them go again. She rummaged in a big bag she had brought.

'See!' she said. 'I have baked you a cake – the sort you loved. And I have chocolate for you too, Viennese chocolate. And for you twins, I have these little dolls from Austria.'

Dear generous Greta. It seemed like old days again to have her there among them. Pam wondered how she could ever have been so hateful to the warm-hearted woman. She looked back to that time, and did not know herself.

Greta looked and looked at Lizzie. 'What's the matter, Greta?' asked Lizzie, laughing. 'Have I changed?'

'Now I know what my friend meant last week when she said to me, "I have seen your pretty Miss Farrell today!"' said Greta. 'I said, "What colour is her hair?" and when she told me I knew it could not be Pamela. But you were not pretty, no, when last I was here. But now you

are vairy, vairy pretty, and you are clever too, so I hear, and Tony, he is almost a man! How you are changed, all of you, but you are my family just the same!'

Sukie screeched, feeling left out in the dining-room. Greta put her hands on her ears. 'Ah, still that parrot squook-squooks,' she said. 'Pamela, you will take some of my cake to your father – it is his favourite!'

The children rushed back with the cake, full of excitement about Greta's return. Aunt Grace laughed to see them, and Sukie squawked in delight. She loved picking the raisins out of a cake.

'Greta's back!' cried Delia.

'Aunt Grace, you're as artful as can be!' said Pam, in a low voice, and twinkled at her great-aunt. 'You kept Greta away till I'd learned my lesson!'

'I've been an interfering old woman!' said Aunt Grace.

'You have!' said Mr Farrell. 'And long may you go on interfering, Aunt Grace – and long may you make your home at House at the Corner!'

'Look at the time!' said Mrs Farrell, suddenly. 'Twins! You really must go to bed! It's shockingly late.'

The twins winked at one another. They had known it was shockingly late for a long time – but it wasn't their business to point it out, with so many grown-ups about! They kissed everyone goodnight, went to bid Greta goodnight too and climbed up the stairs to bed.

'What a wonderful day!' called Delia to David. 'Pam's going to college after all! And Tony's going back to school.'

'And so is Lizzie. And we're going to school together!' shouted back David.

'And Greta's back!' called Delia, stripping off her jersey.

'And we've had a miracle!' shouted David. 'That's the biggest thing of all – a miracle. We've

270

always wanted one and now we've got one. Our prayers came true after all.'

A voice came up the stairs. 'Twins! Will you please stop shouting? We can hear every word you say!'

There was silence after that. Peace descended on House at the Corner. A bumping noise came from the kitchen – Greta at work again. A trickle of song came from there too.

Everything was the same as it had been, but as Aunt Grace looked round, she knew that underneath things were different, quite different.

We aren't all separate now, she thought, separate and pulling against one another. We're one united family, all for one and one for all. That should be our motto. It should be the motto for every family in the kingdom!

Time to pull the blinds down. Nobody can see into the lighted room now. House at the Corner is dark and quiet in the night. Its story is told, its little family is at peace with themselves and one another. All for one and one for all – long may that be their motto!